"We need to talk."

Travis wasn't so easily dissuaded. With gentle fingers he tipped her chin up then kissed her lightly on the mouth. "I was wrong to leave you behind in Vegas."

"You didn't have a choice." Mary Karen's fingers played with a button on his shirt. "You had a plane to catch. So did I."

"If I'd have stayed we could have gotten the marriage annulled. I know how much you wanted to get that done while we were still there."

Her hand dropped. "I'm glad now that we didn't."

Travis frowned. He must be more tired than he realized. Surely she hadn't just said she wanted to stay married.

"Don't get me wrong. I still don't think marriage between us would work," Mary Karen continued as if she'd read his mind. "Unless you've had an epiphany and changed your mind about children?"

Her tone was light but her blue eyes were dark and serious.

"I love your boys, M.K. You know that. But I'm not interested in spending the next twenty years raising children."

"That's what I thought."

"About the annulment. I think—"

"No annulment." Mary Karen shook her head, her gaze now on the full moon. "I'm pregnant."

Dear Reader,

When I wrote the first book in the Rx for Love miniseries, *The Doctor's Baby*, I brought in Mary Karen and Travis as secondary characters. In the next two books, *In Love with John Doe* and *The Christmas Proposition*, they reappeared as part of this close-knit group of friends.

Though I'd initially planned to write only three books set in Jackson Hole, I found there were other characters clamoring for their own stories. At the top of the list were Mary Karen and Travis. I'd developed a soft spot in my heart for the young doctor with the quirky sense of humor and the mother of three very challenging little boys. I wanted to see them get together and have the happy ending they deserved.

I hope you enjoy their love story!

Warmest regards,

Cindy Kirk

If the Ring Fits

CINDY KIRK

MILLS
BOON®
™

First published in Great Britain 2013
by Mills & Boon, an imprint of Harlequin (UK) Limited.
Large Print edition 2013
Harlequin (UK) Limited,
Eton House, 18-24 Paradise Road,
Richmond, Surrey TW9 1SR

© Cynthia Rutledge 2011

ISBN: 978 0 263 23757 3

Harlequin (UK) policy is to use papers that are natural,
renewable and recyclable products and made from
wood grown in sustainable forests. The logging
and manufacturing process conform to the legal
environmental regulations of the country of origin.

Printed and bound in Great Britain
by CPI Antony Rowe, Chippenham, Wiltshire

CINDY KIRK

has loved to read for as long as she can remember. In first grade she received an award for reading one hundred books. Growing up, summers were her favorite time of year. Nothing beat going to the library, then coming home and curling up in front of the window air conditioner with a good book. Often the novels she read would spur ideas, and she'd make up her own story (always with a happy ending). When she'd go to bed at night, instead of counting sheep, she'd make up more stories in her head. Since selling her first story to Harlequin Books in 1999, Cindy has been forced to juggle her love of reading with her passion for creating stories of her own... but she doesn't mind. Writing for the Mills & Boon Cherish series is a dream come true. She only hopes you have as much fun reading her books as she has writing them!

Cindy invites you to visit her website at www.cindykirk.com

To my mother-in-law, Marfae.
Thanks for all your love and support.
You're the best!

Chapter One

The sound of rushing water jolted Mary Karen Vaughn from a sound sleep. Still, she resisted the urge to open her eyes. She'd been having the most delicious dream, and she wasn't ready for it to end. Instead of a quickie—like they'd shared at last year's Christmas party—she and Travis had made love for hours.

She smiled, knowing that was just wishful thinking, er, *dreaming*. Every time she and the handsome doctor had sex it had been fast and furious—a physical release for both of them. He was a bachelor with a busy schedule, and she was a single mom with responsibilities. Both of them had an image in the community to uphold.

Though she knew it wasn't possible, the past couple of times she'd found herself wishing he could hold her for a few more minutes, whisper how beautiful she was just a few more times.

A popular ob-gyn, Dr. Travis Fisher might be one of Jackson Hole's most eligible bachelors but Mary Karen didn't think of him in those terms. He was simply Travis, a dear friend since childhood and a fabulous lover. Back when she was in college, they'd dated a couple of times. She'd really wanted it to work out. But she had wanted a family some day and Travis, well, after helping raise seven younger siblings, he couldn't see kids in his future.

Mary Karen let her eyes drift open. After her divorce they'd renewed their friendship and he'd become her occasional lover. It only made sense he'd play a starring role in last night's mai-tai-fueled dream. Rolling to her side, she realized with a start that she was naked beneath the silk sheets. She smiled. A little rum was obviously a dangerous thing.

It was too bad Trav wasn't here. He'd have enjoyed the view…and gotten all sorts of interesting ideas.

Mary Karen stretched, liking the feel of the sleek sheets against her skin. This vacation had been three days of pure bliss. Most people came to Las Vegas to gamble, but Mary Karen had been content to sit by the pool and read. A couple times guys had tried to pick her up but she wasn't interested. This was her time away from kids and all she wanted was peace and quiet and no distractions.

As she lay, looking at the ceiling, it struck her that the running water had stopped. Earlier she'd sworn that the sound had been coming from her bathroom but had dismissed the ridiculous thought almost immediately. The truth was the walls in the luxurious room on the Las Vegas strip were just way too thin.

Mary Karen's lips quirked upward. Being too thin was a problem she'd like to experience at least once in her life. Although she was still a size six, her belly had a slight pouch and she was more curvy than willowy. Still, for a twenty-six-year-old mother of three, Mary Karen thought she looked pretty darn good…especially now that she'd had some R & R.

After spending the past two days in her new red bikini by the pool, her normally pale skin now had a golden glow.

Winning this trip in a raffle had been just what her body and soul had needed. But today the fun ended. She had to head home in a couple of hours.

While she'd had a wonderful time, she'd missed her sons. And from the hitch in their little voices when she'd spoken with them yesterday afternoon, they missed her, too. But they'd cheered up when she promised she'd be home tonight. With an eleven-o'clock checkout, she needed to get packing.

Pushing back the sheet, she sat up and swung her legs to the side of the bed.

"You're awake."

Mary Karen whirled. She gasped and grabbed for the sheet, pulling it over her breasts.

"It's a little late for modesty, M.K." Travis strolled across the bedroom, clad only in the towel wrapped around his waist, his sandy hair still damp from the shower. "That horse left the barn a long time ago."

Mary Karen could only stare.

At slightly over six feet, Travis was more wiry than muscular. He had a fair complexion with freckles scattered across the bridge of his nose. This morning his hazel eyes, which normally always had an impish gleam, were somber.

He crossed the room and the mattress dipped as he took a seat beside her. Tiny droplets of water still clung to his chest. He smelled like soap and shampoo and that indefinable male scent that sent sparks dancing through her blood.

Then she recalled the rest of last night's dream. A sick feeling filled the pit of her stomach and she began to shake. Could she really have been so foolish? While she'd made some big mistakes in her life, this one would top them all. She'd been buzzed last night but definitely not drunk. Acting out her wildest fantasies in bed with a man she considered her best friend she could handle. But standing before a Bible-wielding Elvis…

Mary Karen searched Travis's face. The despair that suddenly filled his eyes told her what she didn't want to know.

"Tell me we d-didn't." She couldn't quite control the tremble in her voice. "Please, Trav. Tell me we didn't."

Instead of answering he reached over and

lifted her left hand. The emerald-cut yellow diamond on her finger caught the morning light.

"I wish I could say this was one of my jokes." His attempt at a chuckle fell flat.

Her heart thundered in her chest and the room began to spin. "This can't be happening."

"You and I were married last night, M.K," he said, squeezing her fingers. "Now we have to figure out what we're going to do about it."

Four weeks to the day later, Mary Karen left her sons in front of the television with their favorite video playing and locked the door to her home's only bathroom.

She caught sight of herself in the mirror as she placed the sack on the edge of the sink. The hard-won tan from Vegas had already faded and lines of stress edged her eyes. For the past week, she hadn't been able to sleep, worried what this test might show.

For as long as she could remember she'd been

right-on-the-dot regular. A person could set their clock by her menstrual cycle. But when the day she was waiting for came and went just like any other, she knew she was in trouble. Now it was time to know if what she suspected was true. Her hands shook as she completed the test.

Mary Karen could count on one hand the times she'd been truly afraid. The first was when she'd been a child and had wandered away from her parents in Yellowstone. The second had been when Steven had told her he wanted a divorce. The twins had just turned two and she'd been pregnant with Logan. And then there was…now.

The walls of the tiny room closed in around her. A bead of sweat trickled down her spine. Her heart pounded so hard she felt lightheaded. Mary Karen told herself to look at the stick but her eyes refused to cooperate.

Marrying Travis and celebrating with a night of passionate sex had been a crazy thing to do.

She barely remembered how it had happened. One minute they'd been laughing and enjoying a drink by the pool—*one* drink—the next they'd been saying their vows in front of a judge who looked an awful lot like the King of Rock and Roll.

If Travis hadn't been leaving Vegas for his annual medical mission trip, they'd have gotten started on an annulment while they were still in Nevada. Instead she'd had to wait for him to return to Jackson Hole. Now that he was back they could finally work on putting this mistake behind them. What had the attorney she'd contacted said? It would be like the whole thing had never taken place....

Mary Karen took a deep breath and lifted the stick to eye level.

Her heart stopped for several seconds then resumed beating. Louder and more frantically. She tried to tell herself it could be a false positive, but she knew better. She'd been pregnant twice before and the signs were all there. The nausea. The fatigue. The emotional roller coaster.

Tears filled her eyes and slipped down her cheeks. She pushed a bucket of bath tub toys out of the way and turned on the water full force. The last thing she wanted was for her boys to hear her crying and worry.

Dear God, she couldn't have another baby, she just couldn't.

Though it would be easy to make Travis the bad guy, even in her despair Mary Karen knew she had only herself to blame. Fertile Myrtle… that's what her brother laughingly called her. Both of her previous pregnancies had occurred when she'd been on the pill. She should have insisted Travis go out and buy some condoms before she let him touch her.

Stupid. Stupid. Stupid.

She beat her clenched hand against her aching chest and the river of tears turned into a torrent. Breathing grew difficult as a sob blocked her throat.

"Mommy." A small fist pounded on the locked bathroom door. "I hafta go potty."

"Mommy," another childish voice called out. "Open the door. Logan has to go real bad."

Mary Karen swallowed the sob and took a shuddering breath. Her hand fumbled for the box of tissue. She blew her nose and swiped at her eyes before shoving the pregnancy test supplies into the plastic grocery bag. Only after she'd tied the sack shut did she open the door.

"I'm sorry, honey." She stepped aside as her youngest rushed past.

Even though Logan was too focused to pay her much attention, the twins waiting in the hallway were much more observant.

"What's wrong?" With his golden curls and big blue eyes, five-year-old Connor could have been a poster boy for one of God's chosen angels. Until you got close enough to see the devilish gleam in his eyes.

"Your eyes look funny," he said almost accusingly.

"Your face is red," his identical twin, Caleb, chimed in.

"I, I had something in my eye." Mary Karen dabbed the last of the tears away with the tissue clutched in her hand. "Like you did, Cal, last week. Remember?"

"It hurt." Caleb nodded, accepting her explanation without question.

Connor wasn't so easily fooled. His blond brow furrowed and suspicion filled his gaze. "If you got something in one eye, why are *both* your eyes red?"

Instead of answering, Mary Karen dropped her gaze. "You have chocolate on the front of your Spider-Man shirt. Did you get into the M&M's?"

Connor blinked but was spared having to answer when Logan emerged from the bathroom, toilet paper stuck to his sneakers, a big smile on his face. "I went poopy all by myself."

Even though he was three, this was indeed a big deal. After almost five years, her home was finally a diaper-free zone.

But for how much longer? Mary Karen shoved the fear aside and gave her child a hug. "I'm so proud of you."

Logan gave her five seconds before he began to squirm. "Let go." He grunted and pushed back until she released him. "We're playing trucks."

"Okay, you go with your brothers." Mary Karen drew a shaky breath. "Mommy needs to get ready for the party."

Although Travis had returned yesterday from his mission trip in Cameroon she hadn't heard from him. Of course, with her brother, David, hosting a welcome-back barbecue for him tonight, he probably assumed he'd see her then.

Still, she'd expected a call. After all, this marriage mess had shaken them both. Though they were good friends and the sexual energy between them had only grown stronger over the years, they were both smart enough to realize the marriage had been a huge mistake.

She wished it could be different but Travis had been clear—he didn't want children. And she had three of them. Three little boys she adored.

If she ever did marry again, it would be to someone who loved and wanted not only her, but her sons as well. Her ex had taught her a valuable lesson. If love wasn't there in the beginning, if the desire to be a part of a family wasn't there, either, it wasn't going to show up later.

Steven had never wanted to be a husband to her or a father to their boys. She'd tried hard to make their marriage work but from day one he'd blamed her for "trapping" him. And he'd missed no opportunity to throw that in her face. Her heart twisted at the memory.

If Travis found out she was pregnant, he would insist on taking responsibility. He was just that kind of guy. But Mary Karen couldn't let him. She refused to go down that road again. Which meant she was in this alone. Oh, her parents would be supportive. But they were busy with their own lives. And her brother, who'd been such a help when Steven had walked out on her, now had a family of his own. No, the children she had—and any additional children she might have—were her responsibility. Hers and hers alone.

You don't have to have this baby.

The thought was like a whisper on the wind.

Mary Karen refused to let it take hold in her head. She couldn't end this tiny life growing inside her.

"You're a dodo head," she heard Connor yell from the other room.

"Mo-om," Caleb called out. "Connor called me a dodo head."

The words were followed by a crash then the sound of Logan crying.

Mary Karen closed her eyes for a second and took a deep breath. After a heartbeat she opened them, then squared her shoulders and headed for the living room. Later, she'd think about the mess her life had become. For now she had three little boys who needed their mommy.

Travis Fisher pulled his car in front of Dr. Kate McNeal's apartment complex—just a few buildings down from his—and was overcome once again with the feeling that giving her a ride to his welcome-back party was a mistake.

Last night he'd barely gotten into town, when he'd received a call from the hospital. A woman needed an emergency C-section and the other ob-gyns were busy. As the on-call pediatrician, Kate had been in the delivery room.

After the birth, they'd grabbed a quick cup of coffee in the doctors' lounge. They got to talking and she'd mentioned the party.

When she asked if he could pick her up, he hadn't known how to respond. Like she said, she lived close and they were going to the same destination. Riding together made perfect sense. Except he wasn't the guy she'd known before he left for Cameroon. He was…married.

Married. Travis still found it hard to believe. He could only imagine David Wahl's reaction if he heard the news. Though his friend loved to tease his sister, he was her staunchest supporter. No, David would not be pleased.

Thankfully, the annulment would take care of the problem. No one—including David— would ever know.

Travis shut off his BMW Roadster and opened the door. He still couldn't believe he and Mary Karen had been so reckless. The sex he could understand. There'd always been a strong physical attraction between them. But even way back when she was in college and he was in residency, they'd acknowledged that they weren't right for each other. He was live-for-the-moment. She was home-and-hearth.

She was also his best female friend and the one he'd thought of most when he'd been in Cameroon.

Kate stepped out of the front door of her building. He acknowledged her wave with a smile. Though she wasn't as pretty as Mary Karen, Kate was easy on the eyes. Her hair hung to her shoulders in a sleek bob, jet-black and silky. Long dark lashes framed hazel eyes. Tall and lean, she had a fashion sense that made her look more like a model than an up-and-coming pediatrician.

While she didn't make his insides go all crazy like Mary Karen did, Kate was a nice person. There was no reason he should be feeling guilty for giving her a ride. No reason at all. After all, he and M.K. were really married only on paper. The annulment should be as quick as the wedding ceremony.

Travis started up the walk and met Kate halfway. Her summer dress accentuated her willowy figure and full breasts. When he drew close, she opened her arms to him. "I'm so happy you're back."

Obligingly he stepped in and pulled her near, appreciating the clean fresh scent of her. In Cameroon, such common staples like deodorant and toothpaste had been in short supply. Kate was a sweet reminder that he was home. While training other doctors to better help their patients had been a powerful experience, he was very happy to be back.

Kate lifted her face and he realized she expected a kiss. They'd kissed once before he left but this was different. He hadn't been married then. And even if that marriage would be over the second he and Mary Karen had a chance to sign the appropriate forms and let the lawyers do the rest, to participate in even such simple intimacy with another woman felt wrong.

Travis took a step back.

A momentary look of confusion crossed Kate's face. "Is something wrong?"

He smiled and pretended to misunderstand. "Don't want to be late."

Kate started down the sidewalk, and he fell into step beside her. "Will there be people I know at this party?"

"Probably. It will be an eclectic mix. David has invited everyone from colleagues at the hospital to my ski buddy Joel Dennes."

"Joel Dennes?" she asked in a tone that seemed a bit too casual. "The contractor?"

Travis slanted a sideways glance as they reached the car. "You've met?"

"No," she said quickly. "Why would you think that?"

"He has a daughter." Travis shrugged. "I thought she might be one of your patients."

"She may be. I haven't met all the patients in my new practice yet." Her eyes remained focused ahead, her tone noncommittal. "I did meet someone who knows you at the hospital last week."

He opened the passenger side door and helped her into the car. "Who was that?"

"Mary Karen Vaughn," Kate said. "Did you know David Wahl is her brother? I wonder if she'll be at the barbecue."

Somehow Travis managed a smile as he shut her door. "Undoubtedly."

Chapter Two

Mary Karen's brother, David, and his wife, July, had been blessed with a perfect night for their backyard barbecue. The sun shone bright in the blue Wyoming sky. Blooming patches of wildflowers rimmed the large yard. The linen-clad tables had each been adorned with bouquets of sunflowers. For an outdoor event, it felt surprisingly elegant.

"I thought everyone would be dressed a little more casual." Mary Karen glanced down at her blue chambray skirt and scoop-necked lace top, and then back at her friends.

Her sister-in-law, July Wahl, wore a darling tropical-print dress while her friend Lexi Delacorte's cherry-red one-shoulder maternity dress managed to look stylish and comfortable at the same time.

"You look so cute," July said. "I love what you did with your hair."

Mary Karen smiled wryly. "You mean…wash it?"

"Shut up." July gave her a little shove. "I'm talking about pulling it back from your face in those cute little clips."

"I love the look, too," Lexi said. "And, just so you know, we're super jealous of your flat stomach."

"It's hard to be sexy with your belly out in front." July glanced down. "Thankfully, David seems to still find me attractive."

"Nick tells me every day how beautiful I am.

And he's determined to be involved in every aspect of my pregnancy." Lexi's face took on a beautiful glow. "Every morning before he heads into his office, he places a hand on my belly and talks to our son. He read somewhere that listening to the voices of both parents helps the baby feel loved and secure even before he's born."

The vivid image Lexi painted brought a lump to Mary Karen's throat. How different the experience was from her pregnancies. When she was expecting the twins Steve had called her a whale and refused to touch her. Halfway through her pregnancy with Logan, he'd left. Now she'd have to do this alone again. Tears filled her eyes.

She took a sip of iced tea and quickly blinked the moisture back, but apparently not fast enough.

July placed a gentle hand on her shoulder. "Honey, what's wrong?"

"Tell us what has you upset." Concern filled Lexi's amber eyes. "Was it something I said?"

"I'm just tired." Mary Karen forced a smile, knowing at least this was the truth. No matter how much sleep she got at night, it wasn't enough. "The thunderstorms woke Logan. Then the twins heard him, and they were up, too."

She saw no reason to add to the story. When she'd slipped into bed, she'd started thinking what her life was going to be like as a mother of four, and then sleep became impossible.

"I don't know how you do it," July said. "You have three little boys who are bundles of energy. You work—"

"Only part-time," Mary Karen protested, uncomfortable with the admiration she heard in her sister-in-law's tone. She knew many single mothers who had it much worse. At least her ex had a good job and paid his child support on time every month.

Lexi sucked in a breath. "He brought a date."

Mary Karen didn't need to ask who. She'd always had a sixth sense where Travis was concerned. Her heart picked up speed. She lifted her lips in a smile.

But wait. What had Lexi said? A date? Travis had brought…a date?

Her smile wobbled. Bewildered, Mary Karen turned. Her heart gave a leap at the sight of her…husband in khaki pants and a tan-and-blue camp shirt. With his sandy hair bleached a shade lighter than usual and his skin a honey-brown, he looked Tommy Bahama casual and the picture of health. Still, Mary Karen knew him. Perhaps better than he knew himself. She saw beyond the smile on his lips and realized the past four weeks had been tough on him.

Just then a woman's laugh rang out and Mary Karen's gaze darted to Travis's companion. Standing way too close to him, with her fingers resting on his arm in a proprietary gesture, was Kate McNeal. The woman's salmon-and-white jersey dress was a perfect foil for her dark hair and creamy complexion.

While she watched, Kate rose on her tiptoes and kissed Travis's cheek. Mary Karen tightened her fingers around the stem of her glass. Intellectually she understood that she and Travis weren't really a couple. Still, seeing him with Kate was like a knife to her heart. They hadn't even signed the annulment papers and yet it appeared he'd already taken up with a career woman who'd probably never had baby spit-up in her hair.

Lexi took a sip of her club soda and studied the female doctor over the top of her glass. "She's attractive."

"I didn't realize he was seeing anyone." Mary Karen's voice seemed to come from far away. Though only a few minutes earlier she'd felt almost too warm, a chill now settled over her.

July tilted her head, and her gaze turned

thoughtful. "David mentioned they'd gone out a couple times before Travis left for Cameroon."

"He must have called her as soon as he got back," Lexi mused.

Mary Karen thought about last night, how she'd kept her phone close, not wanting to miss his call. Thought about how she'd worried for his safety while he'd been in Africa. Thought about…

Anger bubbled in her veins but she tamped it down, sternly reminding herself that Travis was under no obligation to call her the second he got into town. And it wasn't any of her business if he'd brought a date.

"I swear he's looking for you," July whispered.

"Which is odd considering he's with another woman," Lexi said.

Mary Karen forced her gaze back to the couple and realized her friends were right. When Travis's gaze landed on her, his face brightened.

Ignoring the warmth that rushed through her veins, Mary Karen lifted her hand in welcome, wiggling her fingers.

Obviously taking the gesture as an invitation, he crossed the lawn in several long strides while the statuesque brunette beside him struggled to keep up.

"Welcome back." Mary Karen widened her smile to include the female doctor. "Hello, Kate."

Kate returned the greeting, shifting from one foot to another, looking suddenly as uncomfortable as Mary Karen felt.

"It's good to be home," Travis said, his gaze caressing Mary Karen's face.

Though July and Lexi were standing beside her and Kate lingered behind him, his eyes remained fixed on her alone.

Those hazel eyes were so familiar, so dear, that for a second nothing mattered except that he was home. And safe. And here with her. Until

Mary Karen remembered he hadn't called. And that he was standing in front of her with another woman while she was carrying his child.

The emotional roller coaster she'd been riding since Las Vegas crested the hill. Sudden tears clogged her throat, making speech impossible. Thankfully July and Lexi jumped feetfirst into the conversation, welcoming Kate, asking Travis about his experiences in Cameroon, laughing when he teased them about their huge bellies.

Mary Karen kept her gaze focused on her friends and pretended not to notice Travis's questioning glances. When July and Lexi left to replenish the buffet table, she started to go with them. But they waved her back, assuring her they had the situation under control.

Reluctantly, she plastered a smile on her face and turned back to Travis and Kate.

"Quite a party." Travis gestured with a can

of beer in his hand to the backyard filled with people. "I never knew so many people cared."

"They don't," Mary Karen drawled. "They're here for the free food. And the beer."

Verbally sparring with him was as natural to her as breathing. Their friends knew it, expected it even. But Kate wasn't part of their tight-knit circle of friends.

Kate's eyes widened.

Travis, on the other hand, roared with laughter. "Trust you to put me in my place."

Mary Karen took a sip of tea, her lips curving in a half smile. "Someone has to keep you humble."

"Let me guess." Kate put a finger to her lips, her gaze shifting from Travis to Mary Karen. "Sworn enemies?"

"Close." Travis looped an arm around Mary Karen's shoulders. "Old friends."

His gaze met hers, daring her to disagree.

She couldn't. The woodsy scent she'd come

to associate with him teased her senses and her traitorous body responded to his touch. Seconds later an ache filled her heart at the realization that the easy relationship they'd enjoyed over the years would soon be ending. The rolling in her stomach began in earnest.

"E-excuse me," she stuttered, stepping back from his arms. "I need to…check on something."

Travis called her name but she pretended not to hear. Without a backward glance Mary Karen zigzagged through the crowd. By the time she reached the house, she was running. The bathroom door had barely closed behind her when the crackers she'd eaten this afternoon came up.

It took every ounce of strength she possessed not to break down and bawl. But she'd been here before. She knew the challenges she faced. Being alone and pregnant wasn't for the faint of heart.

She waited for several seconds then slowly

straightened. Still, her body continued to tremble. Mary Karen couldn't help remembering how solicitous her brother had been when July had experienced morning sickness early in her pregnancy. What would it be like to have Travis on the other side of the door waiting, worrying about her?

Stop it.

Mary Karen gave herself a mental shake and rinsed her mouth with unnecessary vigor. After gargling with mouthwash confiscated from below the sink, she squared her shoulders and headed outside to search for her friends.

On the patio, Mary Karen saw her sister-in-law talking to a tall, broad-shouldered man she didn't recognize. July waved her over, then introduced the mystery man as Joel Dennes, a general contractor in the Jackson Hole area. They talked about the rise in home prices before July excused herself.

After chatting with Joel for several minutes

longer Mary Karen noticed people had started pairing up and taking seats for dinner. For the past couple years she'd sat beside Travis at these types of events.

She glanced around the yard and saw Lexi and Nick chatting with him and Kate. Staring at the back of his head, she willed him to turn around and look her way. But his attention remained focused on the lady doctor. Mary Karen's heart gave a ping.

"Food looks good." Joel shoved his hands into his pockets and rocked back on his heels.

Mary Karen refocused her attention on the sumptuous spread. Normally she'd taste a little of everything. Tonight, nothing appealed to her. Still, she knew she had to keep up her strength. If not for herself, for the life growing inside her.

"My friend Lexi did the catering and she's a fabulous cook," she said absently.

By now almost everyone had seated themselves. Kate still stood beside Travis waving her hands, telling some story. A funny one, if their laughter was any indication. Mary Karen turned her gaze back to Joel. "If you're not sitting with anyone, I'd love some company for dinner."

She wasn't sure what made her offer. Maybe it was because he looked as out of place as she suddenly felt. Though she knew everyone here, most of them had someone special with them. Like her, Joel appeared to be flying solo this evening.

He flashed a smile and gestured for her to precede him to the buffet table.

"Amazing." Joel's eyes widened at the variety of food artfully displayed against the brightly covered table linen. "And to think I expected burgers and brats."

"I can vouch for the cucumber gazpacho soup." Mary Karen pointed to an Art Deco–inspired tureen. "It's one of Lexi's specialties."

Joel's gaze dropped to the reddish soup with

brightly colored bits of vegetables and several cucumber curls on top. His easy smile faltered. Instead of reaching for the ladle, he shifted his attention back to her. "Do you have a special dish you like to make?"

"You bet she does," a deep voice responded from behind her. "M.K.'s spaghetti rivals Chef Boyardee."

Mary Karen whirled. "Travis."

Her hope that he'd come to join her for dinner faded when she saw Kate at his side.

Joel grinned and clapped a hand on Travis's shoulder. "Hey, buddy. Welcome back."

"It's good to be home." Travis may have spoken to Joel but his gaze remained firmly fixed on Mary Karen. "I see you've met M.K."

"M.K.? Oh, you mean Mary Karen." Joel slanted a glance in her direction and winked. "We're getting acquainted."

A muscle in Travis's jaw jumped but his smile was easy.

"Would you like to join us?" Joel asked.

"Thanks for the offer but we're already settled in." Kate slipped one arm through Travis's and gestured with the other toward a large table. "The table is already full or we'd ask you to join us."

"Us?" Mary Karen choked out the word.

"Travis and me." Kate spoke slowly as if making a very important point. Or perhaps she thought Mary Karen slow on the uptake. But Mary Karen saw everything all too clearly.

"Of course." Mary Karen could have cheered when her voice came out cool and even, giving no indication of her inner turmoil.

Travis's brows pulled together and his lips pursed. "Actually—"

"That's okay," Mary Karen interrupted. "Joel and I have our eye on that little table by the arbor."

An awkward silence descended.

"You look familiar," Joel said to Kate. "Have we met before?"

"I don't think so." Kate's cheeks pinked. "In fact, I'm almost positive we haven't."

"It's your eyes," Joel continued, for some reason unwilling to let the subject drop. "I know I've seen them."

"I'm going to see if our hostess needs any help." Kate smiled brightly. "I'll see you back at the table, Travis."

With those words, she disappeared into the house.

"I never forget a face." Joel followed her with his eyes. "I just can't place from where."

Not at all interested in talking for even one more second about Kate, Mary Karen smiled and changed the subject. "Do you like lamb, Joel? These burgers with mint and cilantro are very tasty."

"They're *my* favorite," Travis said before Joel could respond.

"Then you should take one." Mary Karen kept her tone light. "But do it quickly. I have a feeling your girlfriend won't like to be kept waiting."

Girlfriend. Even the word tasted bitter on her tongue.

"I don't have a girlfriend," Travis said, his face taking on a mulish expression.

Mary Karen wasn't fooled. And she wasn't in the mood to be generous. "Really? That's not what I've heard."

"Before you left you told me you were dating someone from the hospital." Joel added a large spoonful of pasta salad to his plate. "Did you two split up?"

Travis groaned.

"I think they make a nice-looking couple." Mary Karen elbowed Joel. "Don't you?"

Travis's hazel eyes flashed. Mary Karen told herself she didn't care if she'd ticked him off. She believed in calling a spade a spade.

Still, when Travis flung a lamb burger onto a plate and stalked back to the table where Kate now sat waiting, Mary Karen wondered exactly when it was she'd turned into a jealous fifteen-year-old.

She slapped an extra big dollop of sour cream dill potato salad—that she didn't want—onto her plate pretending it was his head.

Joel didn't seem to mind that the guest of honor had stalked off. Instead, he leaned over and grabbed two bottles of beer from a round silver tub filled with ice and held them up.

Although a Corona sounded surprisingly good, Mary Karen shook her head. It might be only one beer, but she wasn't taking any chances with her baby's health. "Club soda please."

"Thanks for inviting me to sit with you." Joel exchanged one of the beers for a can of club soda. "A pretty woman like you could have her pick of dinner companions."

The compliment was a balm to Mary Karen's battered and bruised ego. Although Joel didn't make her pulse beat faster, with his unruly chestnut hair, brown eyes and rugged features, he was a very attractive man. She quickly discovered he was also a gentleman. When they started across the yard to an empty table, he insisted on carrying her plate.

She'd wondered if once they sat down it would be awkward. After all, they didn't know each other. But conversation flowed easily. By the time they reached for the Key lime pie, Mary Karen had learned Joel had an eight-year-old daughter and that his wife had died of cancer two years earlier. She gave him the abridged version of her own life—minus the new chapter that was about to be written. He seemed genuinely surprised to learn she was divorced and had three small boys.

"You look like a college co-ed." The admiration in his eyes momentary distracted her from her cares.

"I'm twenty-six. But it's nice to know you think I look young and carefree."

Joel brought the beer to his lips, his dark eyes never leaving hers. "You don't feel that way?"

The last time she'd felt unencumbered of life's burdens had been in Vegas…with Travis. And that had turned out so well. Mary Karen gave a strangled laugh.

Joel cocked his head.

"I'm a busy mom," Mary Karen explained, feeling her cheeks burn.

"I understand completely." The handsome contractor leaned forward, resting his forearms on the table. "I come from a family of four boys. There was never a dull moment…or a quiet one. My brothers and I gave my mom fits. But now—except for the gray hairs she blames on us—I know she'd say it was worth it."

"She sounds like a wonderful lady." Mary Karen picked at a loose thread on the tablecloth. "Nowadays so many men—and women—think parenthood is too much work, too much of a hassle."

"You're speaking about your ex." Joel surprised Mary Karen by briefly covering her hand with his. "The man was a fool, Mary Karen. One day he'll wake up and realize that the freedom he wanted so badly wasn't worth all he gave up."

She'd actually been thinking of Travis rather than Steven, but she readily agreed both were fools. Raising three little boys might be challenging at times, but she adored them. She wouldn't trade her chaotic life with them for anything. And, she was certain once this new baby came she'd feel the same way about him. Or her.

Yet life as a single parent wasn't a cakewalk. In fact, most days it was downright tough. And the loneliness... She wasn't sure she'd ever get used to being single in a world of couples. A heaviness wrapped around her heart, the thought of going it alone for the next twenty years was incredibly depressing.

Mary Karen pushed the last few bites of her pie around the plate with her fork for several seconds, then lifted her gaze. "Do you think you'll marry again?"

Joel sat back.

Heat shot up her neck. Dear God, what must he be thinking?

"I'm sorry." She raised both hands, palms to him. "I'm just curious. I'm not shopping for a husband. Honest."

He laughed. "Don't apologize. Even if you were, I'd be flattered."

"But I'm not—"

"No worries." He shot her a wink, and the tenseness in her shoulders eased.

Yes, Joel was a very nice man. It was too bad she wasn't attracted to him. Not that it mattered. Once she was divorced and raising four small children on her own, there would be no time to date.

Mary Karen smoothed the front of her shirt with the flat of her hand. At least Joel still had options.

"So, will you?" she asked. "Marry again?"

Joel shrugged. "If I find the right woman. But she'll have to love not just me, but my daughter as well. Chloe and I, we're a package deal."

"As it should be," Mary Karen murmured almost to herself, thinking of her boys. "Any other way wouldn't work."

"Any other way would be out of the question." Joel's firm tone told her he'd given this matter a lot of thought. "Can you imagine what it'd be like to be a child growing up in a home with a stepparent who wished you weren't there?"

"You're right." Mary Karen slanted a glance in Travis's direction and sighed. "It would never work."

Chapter Three

The sun hung low by the time Travis left the table. With Kate still tagging along, he wandered to the back of the large yard to check out the elk refuge. The familiar rugged landscape of green and brown with the mountains in the distance did little to soothe his jagged nerves. He couldn't get the sadness in Mary Karen's eyes out of his head.

It didn't help knowing he was to blame. What had he been thinking? He should never have agreed to give Kate a lift to the party.

If the pediatrician weren't glued to his hip he could be with Mary Karen right now. Assuring her that she had absolutely nothing to worry about. Confirming that once they completed the annulment papers, what happened in Vegas would forever stay in Vegas.

Oddly, Travis found the thought bittersweet. He remembered how close he'd felt to her the night they'd said their vows. A closeness that had more to do with their friendship and shared history than the mind-blowing sex.

Kate slipped her arm through his, yanking him from his reverie.

"It's beautiful here." Her eyes turned surprisingly somber.

"David and July do have a nice yard," Travis agreed.

"I don't mean just the yard—although it is lovely." Kate slanted a sideways glance in his direction. "I mean Jackson Hole. It's magnificent."

Travis settled his gaze on the land he loved so much. While some people thought of his birthplace only as a place to ski, he knew that was only the tip of what Jackson Hole and the rest of Wyoming had to offer. He casually untangled his arm from Kate's and hooked a boot in the lower rung of the fence. "There's no place like this on earth. Leaving this state was the hardest thing I ever did."

Kate lifted a dark brow. "Why did you?"

Although he'd been old enough to strike out on his own, he'd refused to walk away from his brothers and sisters. Which meant he had to go with them. "I didn't have a choice."

Kate wrapped her arms around herself as if suddenly chilled. "The feeling—that you don't have a choice—is awful."

Travis nodded.

"You went to school in Nebraska, right?"

"I did." Travis spent almost a decade in Omaha. "Great education. Nice people. Awesome college football team. Still, those years seemed endless."

"Medical school and residency are definitely not for the faint of heart," Kate agreed.

Travis chuckled. "School was easy. It was everything else that was hard."

Like the time his sister Margaret had been rushed to the hospital with appendicitis the morning of his Anatomy-Physiology final. She was still in surgery when he'd been called to the high school because his brother Zac had been suspended for fighting.

Kate's gaze grew puzzled. "I don't understand."

He considered making a joke and changing the subject. That's what he usually did when someone asked about his family or something related to his past. But for some reason, he felt like talking tonight. For it all to make sense, he had to start at the beginning.

"Shortly after I graduated from high school,

my parents died in a car accident." Without even realizing what he was doing, Travis dropped into the monotone he used whenever he spoke of his parents' deaths. "Their will made it clear they wanted my uncle in Omaha to raise us if anything happened to them. But Len was a lot younger than my mom and still single. He wasn't sure he was ready for the responsibility."

"I'm sorry about your parents." Sympathy filled Kate's eyes. "Since you went to school in Nebraska, I assume your uncle finally came around?"

He nodded. "We convinced him that all he had to do was provide the house. My sister Margaret and I took full responsibility for our brothers and sisters."

Travis settled his gaze on a herd of bison in the distance and tightened his fingers around the fence post. Prior to his parents' deaths his life had revolved around girls, sports and school. Taking on so much responsibility at such a young age had been a huge change. But he'd seen no other option. "If Meg and I hadn't agreed, Len wouldn't have taken us in and our family would have been split up. My brothers and sisters would have been thrown into the foster-care system."

Kate tilted her head. "How many siblings do you have?"

"Seven."

"No way."

The shock in her voice made him smile. He lifted a hand and pulled his fingers together in an almost-forgotten gesture. "Scout's honor."

Kate's brows pulled together. "I can't imagine how you made it through college and medical school while still fulfilling the promise you made to your uncle."

Her interest appeared genuine, and he was discovering that talking to Kate kept him from noticing how close Mary Karen was sitting to

Joel. Or how pretty M.K. looked with the sun hitting her hair.

"Travis?" Kate prompted.

He pulled his gaze back and focused on the woman at his side. "For starters, I lived at home. I studied while attending sporting events and dance recitals. Thankfully they were good kids. Challenging at times, but a little fire can be a good thing." Travis's lips lifted in a satisfied smile. "Not a slacker in the bunch."

Kate glanced around. "Are any of them here tonight?"

"None of them live in Jackson Hole." Leaving his family in Nebraska to set up practice back here had been hard. But, at that point, they'd all been adults and capable of making their own decision. Still, he hadn't given up hope that they'd all one day find their way back home. "I'm hoping that will change. Even though we live hundreds of miles apart, we're still close."

A thoughtful look blanketed Kate's face.

"With such a successful parenting experience, I'm surprised you don't want kids of your own."

Travis shrugged and watched the sun slip behind a cloud. Until he'd been thrust into the father role, he hadn't realized all that being a parent entailed. He'd felt overwhelmed. Inadequate. Even now he wondered if they'd grown into fine young men and women *in spite* of his efforts and countless rookie mistakes.

He pulled his attention back to Kate and found her staring. But not at him. "What's so interesting?"

"Your 'old friend' and Joel Dennes," Kate blurted out. "They sure seem to be hitting it off."

Travis followed Kate's gaze and frowned. Was his ski buddy holding Mary Karen's hand? Just then she threw back her head and laughed.

A surge of something that felt an awful lot like jealousy stabbed Travis in the side. Usually he was the one making M.K. laugh.

"There's a certain gleam in your eyes when you look at her." Kate's gaze turned sharp and assessing. "Were you lovers?"

She sounded almost hopeful, but that didn't make any sense. Neither did asking something so personal in such a public setting. Thankfully no one was standing close enough to overhear them.

The last thing Travis wanted was to get gossip started. Mary Karen had already endured more than her share. When she'd walked down the aisle six months pregnant with twins, the tongues had started wagging. It had started up again when her jerk of a husband walked out on her when she was pregnant with Logan. The spunky blonde had kept her chin up, but he knew the gossip had stung.

If news about what had happened in Las Vegas got out, M.K. would once again be hurt. But he wouldn't let that happen. He would protect his friend—and her reputation—at all costs.

"You were, weren't you?" Kate pressed. Then her eyes widened. "Don't tell me you two are still dating?"

"Any questions having to do with her are off-limits." His tone made it clear the subject was closed. Still, as they strolled back toward the party, Kate continued to push the issue until he found himself holding on to his temper with both hands.

"You know Kate, it's been a long day." He stopped short of the crowd. "I'm ready to call it a night."

The brunette blinked as if she'd heard the words but they didn't compute. "It's your party. And it's not even ten o'clock."

"David and July will understand." The words came out more clipped than he'd intended, but Travis wasn't about to apologize.

Her gaze searched his eyes.

"I'm sorry, Travis." Kate placed a hand on his arm, two bright spots of pink dotting her cheeks. "Consider me properly chastised. Your relationship with Mary Karen Vaughn is absolutely your business, and none of mine."

The apology brought Kate back up in his estimation but didn't change his mind. Blame it on jet lag and a late night at the hospital, but the party had lost its appeal. He headed across the lawn to where July and David stood, Kate tagging along. By the time he made the rounds and said his goodbyes, the lights were on in the yard and Mary Karen and Joel were nowhere in sight.

Travis briefly considered asking Kate if she'd seen them leave but thought better of it. He kept the conversation on hospital matters until they reached the sidewalk. Kate surprised him by hailing one of her partners who lived in her neighborhood and securing a ride home.

"I can take you," he protested, though perhaps not as strongly as he could have.

She leaned forward and kissed him on the cheek. "I'll see you around."

Although Travis was relieved to watch her go, he insisted on opening her car door, then waited at the curb until the SUV disappeared from sight.

For a second he thought about returning to David's backyard to see if Mary Karen had re-appeared. But the way his evening was going, even if he did find her there'd be no opportunity for them to talk privately. Besides, he was tired. Exhausted. Bone-weary.

After chatting for a few minutes with a couple nurses who'd stopped by specifically to give him a welcome-back hug, Travis headed down the sidewalk. The curb out front had been lined with cars when he'd arrived so he'd been forced to park his new car on a nearby street.

The approaching darkness shrouded the ve-hicle in shadows but as he drew close, the remaining light allowed him to see that someone sat inside.

Not just anyone…

Adrenaline surged. In several long strides he covered the distance to his red BMW convertible. He jerked open the door and slid behind the wheel. "Hey, stranger. I was looking for you."

"I didn't know you bought a new car," Mary Karen said. "Not until David told me."

"It came in right before I left for Cameroon." He gestured with one hand to the luxurious interior. "What do you think?"

"I saw Kate get into Duane's car." She leaned over and straightened the collar of his shirt in a gesture that seemed…wifely. She patted his chest then sat back. "I take it you struck out."

For a moment he thought he'd heard wrong, or that she was teasing…until he noticed her expression. "C'mon. You know me better than that."

"We're only married on paper."

M.K. seemed so tight tonight. But he knew just how to loosen her up. Travis reached over and took her hand, his thumb caressing her palm. "Remember what happened that night, when we returned to the hotel?"

"Umm." She noisily cleared her throat and pulled her hand away. "Yes, there was…that."

"That." Travis trailed a finger up her bare arm. "Was fantastic."

He started humming a few bars of "All Night Long."

"Let me give you a tip." While he was still humming, Mary Karen leaned close so that her lips touched his ear. "Bringing a date to the party then talking dirty to me is not a way to score points."

The tune died in his throat. Was she serious? Travis straightened, his gaze searching hers. It appeared he had some explaining to do. "Kate wasn't my date, M.K. She lives near me and asked if I'd give her a ride. That's it. Nothing more."

Mary Karen crossed her arms, clearly not convinced. "It looked like a little more than that to me."

"Then you need glasses." His attempt to lighten the mood fell flat. "She's only a friend."

Mary Karen lifted a brow. "A friend with benefits?"

"Without," he snapped. "I'm not sleeping with her, M.K. I wouldn't do that."

"I'm not sure I believe you." Mary Karen held his gaze and flipped a strand of long blond hair over her shoulder. "Joel said you'd been dating Kate before you left for Cameroon and—"

"Joel Dennes needs to get his facts straight." Travis spoke between gritted teeth. "Kate and I went out for drinks a couple times with a group from the hospital. That's the extent of our 'dating.'"

"You brought her to the party," M.K. pointed

out. "You never bring girlfriends to these types of gatherings. What am I to assume except... she must be special."

Travis had never seen this side of Mary Karen. It was almost as if she were jealous. But that didn't make sense. He opened his mouth to tell her it wasn't any of her business—in a nice way, of course—when he realized with a jolt that it was her business. Just like he hadn't liked seeing her with Joel, she hadn't liked seeing him with Kate.

She was his wife.

He was her husband.

The second they'd signed that marriage license, the rules had changed. Which meant he owed her more of an explanation. *And,* an apology.

"I ran into Kate at the hospital last night," he said. "David had invited her to the party and she asked me to pick her up. I should have said no."

"Hmm." Mary Karen brought a finger to her

lips. "You had time to talk to Kate about the party, yet you didn't have time to call and let me know you'd gotten back safely."

Instead of being angry for being called onto the carpet once again, Travis found himself admiring Mary Karen's spunk.

"You're absolutely right," he said. "I should have called."

Surprise flitted across her face as if his response had taken her by surprise. "Y-yes," she stammered. "You should have."

"Do I need to grovel?" It was an old joke between them. Some offenses required not just an apology, but some serious groveling.

A smile tugged at her lips before she brought her mouth under control. She pretended to think for a moment, then nodded. "Because of the multiple infractions, groveling will be required."

Thankfully he was in the car. If it were anywhere else, she'd probably have made him get down on his knees. He clasped her left hand between his. "I'm sorry, M.K. I really am. I'm a thoughtless, despicable ass. If you forgive me, I swear the next time you make your tofu pizza, I'll eat it and you won't hear a word of complaint. That's how truly sorry I am."

She pretended to ponder his words but her smile reappeared.

"Apology accepted," she said with a decisive nod. "And I'll hold you to that tofu pizza promise. Don't think I won't."

"I missed you. As the words left his lips he realized they were true. "Did you miss me?"

Mary Karen lifted a shoulder in an exaggerated shrug. "I may have thought about you once or twice."

"Brat." Relief washed over him. He smiled then reached for her. Before she could protest and pull away, he pressed his mouth to hers.

Surprise was on his side. She instantly softened against him. Her fingers slid through his hair as they continued to kiss, long passionate kisses that sent fire coursing through his body. Then, abruptly, just as his hand slid beneath her shirt, she pulled away and glanced around.

"Discretion, Trav," she said, sounding breathless, her lips swollen from his kisses, her hair tousled.

Travis groaned. *Discretion* had been their byword since they'd started their friends-with-benefits relationship three years ago. The rules were simple. No hugs or kisses where they could be seen by others. Other than last year's Christmas party where a plethora of mistletoe had caused things to get a bit out of control, they'd stuck to those rules.

"You're no fun," he grumbled.

The rarely seen dimple in her left cheek flashed. "That's what my boys tell me."

"If you insist on privacy…" Travis slid the key into the ignition and the engine purred.

"Where are we going?" she asked.

"Someplace private," he said. "Where we can talk and not be disturbed. Is that okay with you?"

She thought for a moment, her eyes dark and unreadable in the dim light. Then she nodded. "We do need to talk."

Conversation wasn't exactly what Travis had in mind. He wanted to hold her close, feel her body respond to his, reassure himself that their temporary marriage hadn't changed things between them. But if she wanted to talk, they would talk.

She reached forward, switching radio stations. He wasn't surprised when she stopped the search when she got to a country one. He knew her tastes as well as he knew his own.

Travis put the car in gear but didn't hit the gas. Instead he let his gaze linger, watching the way the light from the moon caught the golden blond of her hair. Pretty, intelligent and with a heart as big as the Wyoming sky. No wonder no other woman held a candle to her.

The strains of a steel guitar filled the cab and she sat back with a satisfied sound. Travis pulled away from the curb and relaxed fully for the first time since he'd left for Cameroon.

He turned onto US 26, passing the four antler arches in the town square. Surprisingly, for someone who'd wanted to talk, M.K. didn't seem to have much to say. So Travis picked up the ball and ran with it, just like he had in high school when he'd been the running back and had taken a handoff from David.

Travis told Mary Karen about the baby he'd delivered last night, how concerned he'd been when he'd first arrived at the hospital, his relief when all went well. Once he turned onto the highway the talk shifted to Cameroon and his time in the East Region.

He could still see the men grilling fish and soya and brochette over homemade barrel grills at the side of the roads. Then, the talk turned professional. As a nurse, Mary Karen could appreciate the challenges of providing medical care in hospitals without running water.

She listened attentively, occasionally making encouraging noises.

"I'm never going to complain about anything again," he vowed, turning off the highway onto a side road. "We have so much here, so much to be thankful for."

"I'd thought about going into the Peace Corps when I got out of college." Mary Karen's eyes took on a faraway look. "As a nurse, I knew I could be of real help to those less fortunate."

Peace Corps? Mary Karen? He'd dated her when she'd been in college. She'd been the pretty sorority girl who always had a smile on her face. This volunteer thing was news to him. "Why didn't you do it?"

The smile on her lips vanished. "C'mon, Trav. You know why."

Then he remembered. Her senior year she'd begun dating Steven, a man without an altruistic bone in his body. By the time she'd graduated with her Bachelor of Science in Nursing, she'd been five months pregnant.

Travis pulled off the highway onto a rarely used dirt road and parked the convertible.

"You never told me about the Peace Corps thing." For some reason not knowing bothered him. They were friends. He knew what radio stations she liked. He knew her favorite flavor of ice cream. Shouldn't he also have known she'd once considered going into the Peace Corps?

He motioned her closer. When she leaned in, he slipped an arm around her shoulder and nuzzled her hair. The familiar scent of strawberries teased his nostrils. "You smell good."

"None of that." She pressed a hand against his chest and pushed him back. "We need to talk."

Travis wasn't so easily dissuaded. With gentle fingers he tipped her chin up then kissed her lightly on the mouth. "First let me say I'm sorry."

Her eyes were large and luminous. "For what?"

Both of his arms were around her now. He pulled her close and felt her heart fluttering like a hummingbird against his chest. "I was wrong to leave you behind in Vegas."

"You didn't have a choice." Mary Karen's fingers played with a button on his shirt. "You had a plane to catch. So did I."

"If I'd have stayed we could have gotten the marriage annulled." He wondered if she was worried that he would drag his feet getting the papers filed. "I know how much you wanted to get that done while we were still there."

Her hand dropped. "I'm glad now that we didn't."

The words were soft but still audible. Travis frowned. He must be more tired than he realized. Surely she hadn't just said she wanted to stay married?

"Don't get me wrong. I still don't think marriage between us would work," Mary Karen continued as if she'd read his mind. "Unless you've had an epiphany and changed your mind about children?"

Her tone was light but her blue eyes were dark and serious.

In Cameroon he'd had a lot of time to think. During the long hot nights he'd wondered what it'd be like if they stayed married. But each time he'd come to the same conclusion. What he wanted and what she wanted were too far apart. "I love your boys, M.K., you know that. But I'm not interested in spending the next twenty years raising children."

"That's what I thought."

"About the annulment. I think—"

"No annulment." Mary Karen shook her head, her gaze now on the full moon.

Travis wondered if she was worried that getting the annulment would cost money she didn't have. But that couldn't be it. He'd assured her that he'd pay for it. Perhaps—

"I'm pregnant."

The breath froze in Travis's throat. "Beg pardon," he returned, keeping his expression perfectly still.

"I'm pregnant." Her fingers twisted in her lap. She lifted her gaze to his and he saw the truth in the tears shimmering in her eyes.

When Travis had been ten his brother had hit him in the chest with a two-by-four, forcing all the air from his lungs. To this day he remembered that awful, panicky feeling. He felt the same way now.

After a long moment, he cleared his throat. "Are you sure?"

"I did a home test. It came back positive." She chewed on her lower lip. "I have all the symptoms."

He had to be in an alternate universe. There could be no other explanation. "You're on the pill."

Then he recalled why her brother called her Fertile Myrtle. Both times she'd gotten pregnant before, she'd been on oral contraceptives.

"I should have used a condom." A sick feeling took up residence in the pit of his stomach. "We'd always used one before."

"Yeah, well…" Her voice trailed off and he saw the despair in her eyes.

"Are you planning on having the baby?" He tried to keep his tone casual. Although this was his child she was carrying, he was well aware that this was ultimately her choice.

"Are you asking me to have an abortion?" Her voice rose then broke.

"Nononono." He reached for her hand. "How could you possibly think that?"

Mary Karen jerked her hand away and crossed

her arms. "You don't like children. You told me that yourself less than five minutes ago."

"Of course I like children. I'm an obstetrician. I bring children into the world on a daily basis." As he spoke, Travis tried to remember his earlier words. "I merely said I didn't want to raise them."

Tears spilled from her lids and slid down her cheeks.

Damn. He was an intelligent man, but that didn't seem to stop him from putting his foot in his mouth.

"Ah, M.K." He pulled her against him despite her protests. "It'll be okay. Don't cry."

"I'm not crying," she said between sobs. "Crying is s-stupid."

"No, it's not," he said in a soothing tone. As he stroked her hair, he realized this wasn't just about him. He'd put his best friend in an untenable position.

"I'm getting your shirt wet." She tried to pull away, but he tightened his hold.

"I don't care about the shirt." He leaned his forehead against her hair. "I care about you."

It was the truth yet something he'd never said to her before. Though they'd been as intimate as two people could be, they'd always been careful to avoid talking about feelings.

"Caring doesn't matter." Mary Karen pulled a tissue from her purse and blotted her eyes. "Steven cared about me. Look how that turned out."

Steven was also an arrogant, self-centered jerk. From the moment he'd set foot in Jackson Hole, Travis hadn't liked the guy. And he certainly hadn't appreciated the way he'd treated Mary Karen.

"This is such a big mess." She sniffed then blew her nose.

Big mess seemed a bit mild, considering the impact, but Travis agreed with the assessment.

They'd stay married. What other choice was

there? Mary Karen was his friend. She was carrying his baby.

Travis blew out a harsh breath. It looked like he was about to become a family man…whether he wanted to or not.

Chapter Four

Mary Karen pushed back from Travis's arms. It wouldn't do to get too comfortable. She'd told him about the baby. She'd accomplished her goal for the evening.

"The lease on my apartment will be up next month," he said, thinking outloud. "Since your place is bigger, I'll move in with you. After the baby is born, we can talk to Joel about building a house for us."

The resignation in his eyes made her heart clench. It mirrored what she'd seen in her ex-husband's eyes when she'd told him she was pregnant.

"No," she said softly, then repeated more loudly as if to convince herself, "no. You're not moving in with the boys and me."

"What are you talking about?" Confusion blanketed Travis's handsome features. "Of course I'm moving in. You need me. Now more than ever."

Mary Karen briefly closed her eyes and prayed for strength. She did need him. Or rather she needed a partner on this scary journey. But a willing partner, not one who was only with her because he felt obligated.

But wasn't having someone *better than being alone?* a tiny voice in her head whispered.

No. She wouldn't do that to herself again. Or to Travis. If she brought him with her down this familiar road, there'd be pain at the end for everyone. For him. For her. Most significantly for her children. "You don't want to be married or have a family."

Travis didn't bother to argue the point. How could he? He'd made his feelings on marriage and children very clear on many occasions. What had he told her at Christmas? Being married and having children would be like a noose around his neck.

He wiped a weary hand across his face. "M.K., you and I both know life isn't simply about what we want. Honor and duty matter, too."

Though his words only confirmed what she already knew, they were like a dagger to her heart. "I married one man because I was pregnant," she said in a quiet tone. "I won't make that mistake again."

Travis gave a half-hearted chuckle. "It's a good thing I have a strong ego or being lumped into the same category as your ex might cause me some serious psychological trauma."

He reached over and cradled her ice-cold fingers in his strong ones. "C'mon, it won't be so bad. Your parents like me. Your brother is my best friend. And your kids think I'm cool."

Her children. "They won't think you're so cool when you get tired of us and leave."

"Stop with the comparisons to your ex." Travis's hazel eyes flashed. "Leaving is Steven's M.O., not mine."

"I apologize." She'd been wrong to lump him in with her ex. Mary Karen knew in her heart that he'd stick around but at what cost? Oh, he'd try to hide his unhappiness. But she knew him so well, she'd see right through his act. And while she knew he'd be good to her boys, wouldn't they eventually pick up on the fact that his heart wasn't in being a father?

No, having him move in wasn't an option. But what were they going to do? And how would they explain it all to their family and friends? Time, she needed a little more time. "Promise me you won't say anything about our marriage or the baby to anyone. Not just yet."

"You won't be able to hide your pregnancy for long," Travis pointed out. "After three children—"

"I know." She didn't need anyone to remind her that all too soon she'd resemble a beached whale. "It's just that I want time before—"

"—everyone finds out you took the biggest player in Jackson Hole off the market and got knocked up in the process?"

In spite of the seriousness of the topic, Mary Karen had to chuckle. Trust Travis to put his own unique spin on things. "Something like that."

"I wouldn't want anyone to know I'd married me, either," he said in a conversational tone, looping an arm companionably around her shoulders. "But I think it's better they know sooner rather than later."

Normally she would agree. But not in this situation. Mary Karen had the feeling no one was going to be happy or agree with her decision. "Just keep it quiet for now. Okay?"

"I'll go along with whatever makes it easier for you," Travis said, but he didn't look happy.

"I'd also like to postpone the divorce until after the baby is born." Mary Karen swallowed hard against an unexpected lump in her throat. Poor sweet baby didn't deserve all this drama.

"Divorce?" Travis's eyes widened and a rarely seen muscle in his jaw jumped. At the same time, his brows slammed together. "I thought that was off the table."

"I never said that." She shifted her gaze into the darkness over his shoulder. "Neither of us want to stay married. Not really."

"But you're pregnant."

Mary Karen sighed. "Believe me, I'm well aware of that fact."

Without warning Travis pushed his door open and stepped from the vehicle.

"What are you doing?" Mary Karen asked.

"I'm going for a walk." Travis rounded the front of the car and opened her door. "With you."

When he held out his hand, she hesitated for only a second before placing her fingers into his firm grasp and stepping from the warmth of the car into the cool night air. The stones of the gravel road crunched beneath her sandals.

She hadn't even had a chance to shut her door when a gust of wind swept across the open countryside, ruffling her hair and making her shiver. Mary Karen wrapped her arms around herself. Perhaps going for a walk wasn't such a good idea.

Travis paused. Then he bent down and reached under the seat, rummaging around.

"I know it's here somewhere." Finally, with an exclamation of triumph, he pulled out a wrinkled gray hoodie. "Just what the doctor ordered."

Though the jacket looked a bit tattered, when he offered it to her Mary Karen wasn't about to argue. She slipped her arms into the soft, warm fleece and Travis zipped it up with a solicitousness that brought tears to her eyes.

Just for a second, she let herself wonder what it'd be like if Travis loved her and wanted to raise children and grow old with her for all the right reasons. She breathed in the faint scent of the cologne that clung to the fabric and wished with all her heart that things could be different.

"Warm enough now?" he asked.

She nodded and ducked her head, afraid of the longing he might see in her eyes.

"Good." He took her arm and crooked it through his. "Now, tell me why you won't give me, us, a chance."

Mary Karen looked up. The moon hung large in the sky. A zillion stars sparkled brightly overhead. But romance and love were no longer in those stars for her. She thought of the other dreams she'd once clung to, the hopes she'd had of making a difference in the world. Those fantasies were now out of reach, too. Sadness engulfed her heart.

It would be so easy to let Travis move in. It would certainly make her life easier. But her boys' welfare had to be her priority. A father who didn't want to be one would only hurt them in the end.

She felt his curious gaze on her as they walked down the deserted stretch of road.

"M.K.," he said. "I want to do right by you."

Of course he did. Despite his somewhat hedonistic lifestyle, Travis Fisher was an honorable man. When he'd been a teenager, he'd made the sacrifices necessary to keep his family together. Now he was once again willing to sacrifice the life he'd always wanted because he'd gotten her pregnant.

But as fearful as Mary Karen was of raising four children alone, she was more afraid of being in another marriage based on duty and obligation, not love.

Just like she wanted more for Travis, she wanted more for herself and her boys.

If she said that to him, he'd assure her they'd make it work. That's what Steven had said, too. Until making it work had become too onerous and he'd wanted out.

"M.K.? Let me be a part of your life."

Mary Karen stifled a groan. She knew Travis. He wouldn't stop until he'd convinced her.

"I have my standards, Trav," she said softly, taking a step closer, crowding him. She lifted her hand and brushed a strand of hair back from his forehead. "I could never be with a man who cheats at poker."

Travis's eyes, which had darkened with passion, cleared and he chuckled. "It was strip poker. And you wanted that last piece of lingerie off as much as I did."

She waved a hand. "So you say."

But he caught her eye and they shared a smile.

Mary Karen resumed walking and Travis fell into place beside her. After several steps he cast a sideways glance. "Have you thought about who you'll see for your OB care?"

Something about the way he asked the question made her suspicious. "Please don't tell me you're thinking of volunteering?"

"Well, I am the best." The dimple in his cheek flashed. "But it'd be a conflict. You saw Tim Duggan for Logan. He'll do a good job."

The mere thought of walking into Travis's practice, where she knew all of the doctors and most of the nurses made Mary Karen break out in a cold sweat. "I'm sure he would, but I was actually thinking of going to that new woman OB in town."

"But we're the premiere group in Jackson." A frown furrowed Travis's brow. "Why would you want to go anywhere else?"

"I walk into your clinic pregnant with your

baby…and it will be all about you. What kind of delivery *you* think is best, how *you* think the pregnancy is progressing," Mary Karen whispered although there was no one for miles. "What I want, what I feel, won't even matter."

Her voice broke. Yet, even as the words were leaving her lips, she'd known they weren't true. Travis wasn't that kind of guy. He wouldn't take over and run the show. But how could she explain that picking the doctor was something she needed to do to show she was in control of some part of her life?

For a long moment, Travis didn't speak. She knew he was surprised. After all, Tim had delivered Logan. Why would she switch now? And to a doctor who wasn't even part of his group. She braced herself for an argument.

"I've heard good things about Dr. Kerns," he said finally.

"You're okay with me seeing her?"

"Do I have a choice?" His smile took any sting from the words.

"Of course you do," she said, her defenses breached by his easy acquiescence. "This is your baby, too."

"But it's your body." His expression had turned serious. "If seeing Dr. Kerns will make this pregnancy easier for you, I'm all for it."

Her heart did a slow roll just as the alarm on her phone went off. Mary Karen glanced at the readout then back up at him. Normally her brother or her parents watched her children on the rare occasions when she went out. But tonight a high school girl was babysitting. She'd warned the boys to be nice, but didn't hold out much hope. "I'm sorry but we're going to have to go back. I promised the babysitter I'd be home by eleven."

"No worries." He crooked his arm and she slipped her hand through it. "It's been a long day for both of us."

They turned around and headed back to the car. By the time they reached the vehicle, the wind had picked up. Mary Karen slipped inside as soon as Travis opened the door.

After buckling her seat belt, she rested her head against the seat, suddenly fighting an overwhelming sense of fatigue. Warmth soon flooded the small vehicle wrapping itself around her like a favorite blanket. She closed her eyes for just a moment. When she opened them, Travis was pulling the car to a stop in front of her home.

"Sorry. I guess I'm a little tired," she mumbled, letting her heavy lids drift shut again.

Travis chuckled. "I'd never have guessed."

A moment later she felt a hand on her shoulder and a gentle shake. "C'mon, sleepyhead."

Forcing her eyes open, Mary Karen stumbled out of the car. Travis took her arm, ignoring her protests. They'd barely stepped onto the porch when the door flung open. Erin, the sixteen-year-old babysitter, motioned them inside.

Dressed in skinny jeans and an oversize cotton sweater, belted at the waist, the girl looked as if she could be in college instead of high school. Her family lived just down the street and she'd offered to watch the boys before, but the timing had never been right.

"Mrs. Vaughn, I did my best. I really tried." The girl brushed a strand of hair back from her face, her cheeks as bright as her hair.

"What happened?" Mary Karen asked, a sick feeling filling the pit of her stomach. Unlike some mothers who seemed to be in a permanent state of denial about their children's behavior, she operated under no such illusions.

"Logan was an angel. He's been asleep since eight. But Connor and Caleb, well, they wouldn't listen. They refused to go to bed. They even hid my chemistry book. It took me forever to find it." For a second tears filled Erin's large green eyes but she blinked them back. "And I have a test tomorrow."

"I'm so sorry." Mary Karen rested a hand on the girl's shoulder, conscious of Travis standing beside her, taking it all in. If it was anyone else but him, she'd have been embarrassed to have them hear about her misbehaved children. But Travis had twin brothers. *Double trouble* weren't just words to him. "You shouldn't have to put up with that kind of behavior. Did they finally go to bed for you?"

Before Erin could respond, a large black-and-white cockapoo appeared in the foyer flanked by two little boys in identical red cartoon pajamas.

"I think that's a no." A smile played at the corners of Travis's lips.

"Hi, Mommy." Connor gave a little wave. "Hi, Travis."

"Can we have a snack?" Caleb asked.

Mary Karen swallowed a groan.

Erin leaned close and spoke in a conspiratorial whisper. "They've already had two snacks."

The babysitter's perfume was a cloying floral scent and so strong the girl must have just spritzed it on. Mary Karen's stomach lurched. She breathed through her mouth, fighting the urge to gag. When she realized she was losing the battle, she pressed her fingers to her lips and rushed from the room, a barking dog on her heels.

Over the boys' curly heads, Travis met Erin's confused gaze. He didn't have a clue what had made M.K. move so quickly until he caught a whiff of Erin's perfume. Then he understood. Pregnant women were notoriously sensitive to odors, er, scents.

"You check on Logan," Travis called after Mary Karen, though she'd already disappeared down the hall. "I'll take care of things here."

"Logan is asleep." A tiny frown furrowed Erin's brow. "He's fine."

"You know how mothers can be." Travis reached into his pocket and pulled out several large bills. "Will this be enough?"

The girl's eyes widened. "Wow. Yeah. More than enough."

"Consider it combat pay," Travis said. "I'm sure you earned every cent."

"Thank you, Dr. Fisher." Erin glanced nervously at the twins who stood staring intently at her. She tossed her bag over her shoulder, grabbed her jacket from the coat tree and inched toward the door. "Should I stick around to speak with Mrs. Vaughn or is it okay if I leave?"

"I'm going to tell Mommy you were mean to me. You wouldn't let me put chocolate on my ice cream," five-year-old Connor said in an accusing tone.

"Yeah," Caleb echoed, his lip jutting out. "You were super mean."

"Enough." Travis stepped forward and clamped a hand on each boy's shoulder, not letting go even when they began to squirm. "Erin, thanks again for watching the children. I know they can be a challenge."

The girl edged her way to the door, keeping the boys in sight. "They've got a lot of energy."

"Say thank you to Erin, boys." His tone brooked no argument. The girl had obviously gone through hell tonight. At the very least she deserved a little politeness at the end of the evening.

Caleb kicked the carpet with his toe. "Thank you."

Travis fixed his gaze on Connor.

"Thank you," the other twin finally echoed.

Travis stood by the door with the boys and watched until the girl was safely in her house across the street.

"I didn't like her," Connor said. "I'm glad Mommy's home."

"Where'd Mommy go?" Caleb's gaze scanned the room.

"Your mother isn't feeling well." Travis had planned to head home, put up his feet and have a cool one. He had a lot to think about. But he couldn't turn these two loose on M.K. After all, she wouldn't be in the bathroom throwing up if it wasn't for him. "I'll be tucking you in tonight."

Connor's expression brightened. "Will you tell us a monster story?"

His twin shoved him. "T. rex story."

Connor took both hands and pushed his brother back. Hard. "Monster story."

Travis separated the two before the childish sparring turned into a full-blown fight then herded them to their bedroom. He wasn't sure what snacks they'd consumed but based on how they were behaving, he'd guess the treats contained lots of sugar and caffeine. By the time he'd gotten them tucked in and made up both a monster *and* a dinosaur story, he decided he should have given Erin another twenty.

With the two finally sleeping peacefully, he went in search of their mother. He'd heard M.K. in the bathroom when he'd passed by earlier, but now that door was open, which Travis took to be a positive sign.

He found her in her bedroom, asleep on the bed, her clothes and shoes still on. Travis slipped the heeled sandals off, then covered her with the knitted throw she always kept neatly folded over a chair.

She looked so young lying there with her blond hair spread out around her face; Mary Karen was a beautiful young woman who should be worrying about nothing more important than the next party to attend.

Now, because of him, she'd be raising not three rambunctious children, but four. He set his jaw. Regardless of what Mary Karen thought, they were in this together. She would have his help, whether she wanted it or not.

Chapter Five

The next two weeks passed quickly. Travis wanted to be with Mary Karen but it seemed every time he called she was too busy to talk for very long. The only time he got to see her was at the hospital. She told him she was trying to get in the nursing hours while she still could work.

His life had shifted into high gear, too. While he'd been gone, his partners had picked up the slack. Now a couple of them had taken some well-deserved vacation time, which left him to fill in for them.

Like today, it was barely 5:00 p.m. and he'd already delivered his third baby. The first two women had their husbands with them in the delivery room. The last patient had been a college student. The girl had stayed strong but he'd seen the fear in her eyes. It didn't seem right that any woman should have to go through pregnancy and childbirth alone.

Mary Karen's first prenatal appointment with Dr. Kerns was scheduled for next week. She'd let that little bit of information slip in their brief telephone conversation last night. He'd offered to rearrange his schedule and go with her but she'd told him not to bother.

Not to bother? Did she ever once consider that he might want to share the experience with her? But when he'd tried to explain that he *wanted* to be there, he'd heard a crash. She'd told him Connor had broken the cookie jar and she had to get off the phone and clean it up. He'd asked her to call him back, but he hadn't heard from her.

Travis barely noticed the staff in the halls on his way to the doctor's lounge. Instead of the exhilaration he normally felt after bringing a new life into the world, it was as if a huge weight had settled on his shoulders. For some reason, his wife—his pregnant wife—wanted nothing to do with him.

He couldn't help picturing M.K. in that office tomorrow, seeing her baby—their baby—for the first time on that ultrasound screen… and being alone.

When he reached the lounge he was relieved to find it empty. Though Travis normally liked connecting with colleagues, today he didn't feel like making small talk. Ignoring the coffee and fruit that had been set out by hospital volunteers, he passed through a second door into the locker area. Though he should be thinking about his car or his fantasy football picks, all he could think about was how he'd failed Mary Karen.

While he didn't want to harass her or make her life more difficult, he couldn't let her go to her appointment without him. No, tonight he would call and insist—

Without warning, Travis found himself slammed against a locker with such force it pushed most of the air from his lungs.

"You bastard." David's face came into view, his eyes dark with anger. "She was finally getting her life together. How could you do this to her?"

Travis didn't need to ask what "this" was. His friend had obviously found out his sister was pregnant…and that Travis was the father. Grabbing hold of his anger with both hands, Travis shoved David back. "It wasn't like we planned it. It just happened."

"Don't give me that." Disappointment filled David's blue eyes. "I've seen the way you act around her. Do you think I didn't notice you sneaking into that bedroom with her at the Christmas party? I thought you'd be smart enough to take precautions. Mary Karen does not need another baby to raise."

"That's true." In fact, Travis couldn't agree more. But that didn't change the facts.

"You're taking responsibility." David set his jaw at a hard angle. "You're marrying her."

Travis resisted a nervous urge to laugh. But he suppressed it, knowing if he did David would deck him. Though his friend and M.K. had done their share of arguing growing up, David loved his sister deeply and was extremely protective of her. When her ex had left town, it had been her parents and David who'd been left to pick up the pieces.

"Mary Karen and I are already married, David." Travis tried to ignore the latch of the green metal locker digging into his back. "We were married in Vegas before I left for Cameroon. The baby she's carrying was conceived on our wedding night."

Surprise flashed across his friend's face followed quickly by relief. David's hands dropped to his side and took a step back. "I—I didn't know. July told me Mary Karen started crying when they met for lunch and when she asked what was wrong, Mary Karen told her she was pregnant. She didn't tell July she was married."

As Travis straightened, he saw the puzzlement in his friend's eyes…and the hurt. David didn't understand why Mary Karen hadn't confided in him. Or why he, supposedly David's best friend, hadn't shared that information.

"We were going to get the marriage annulled… the whole 'what happens in Vegas, stays in Vegas' thing," Travis explained. "The baby changed those plans."

David's eyes darkened with suspicion.

"If you're married, why did you bring Kate to

the party? And why aren't you and Mary Karen living together?"

"I gave Kate a ride. That's all. And your sister won't let me move in," Travis said, oddly embarrassed by the admission. "She's worried about the boys. She thinks I'll eventually leave her, leave them, like Steven did."

"You're not anything like him." David's tone made it clear what he thought of his former brother-in-law. "Surely she realizes that."

"I'm not sure what's going on in her head." Travis blew out a frustrated breath. "Not only won't she let me move in, she's insisting that after the baby comes, she's divorcing me."

"Whoa, cowboy." David raised a hand. "Divorce? You just got married."

"I'm very aware of that fact," Travis snapped.

David's brows pulled together. "Is it you who wants the divorce?"

Didn't his friend understand it had stopped

being about what he wanted the second he'd found out she was pregnant?

"I want to take care of her and our baby," Travis said through gritted teeth. Though it didn't seem quite real yet, by Christmas his son—or daughter—would be here. "I've tried to convince her to let me be a part of her life but she refuses. Your sister is extremely stubborn."

"Tell me about it." David chuckled then quickly sobered. "Listen to me, Trav. You can be charming and persuasive when you set your mind to it. Set your mind to getting back in her good graces. Convince her to let you back into her life. Don't let her down."

An obvious warning underscored the words, but David's threats had no impact other than to make Travis realize it was time to pull out all the stops. December wasn't that far away.

He knew what needed to be done. While he didn't like to be anything less than honest, desperate times called for desperate measures.

"Don't worry, bro." Travis stood and put a hand on his friend's shoulder. "Mary Karen may not want me to be her husband right now. But she will. Trust me, she will."

Ever since she'd been a little girl, Mary Karen had loved the beginning of summer. One of the reasons was that it heralded the arrival of the farmer's market in Jackson. Produce vendors, as well as booths selling homemade crafts and fresh flowers, took over the downtown sidewalks every Saturday morning. Today it was lettuce, asparagus and wild mushrooms that had made Mary Karen hop out of bed extra early.

Though she did not consider herself by any stretch of the imagination to be a cook, for the sake of her children's health, she tried. And since she had a black thumb, that meant picking up fresh vegetables from someone else's garden whenever she had the chance.

She brushed a strand of hair from her face

with the back of one hand and waited for the grandmotherly-type to stuff the organic lettuce into a bag. A trickle of sweat traveled down her spine. When she'd gotten up, it had been a cool thirty-seven degrees outside. That's why she and the boys had worn coats for the short morning walk. Unfortunately now that the sun was high in the sky, it had to be close to seventy.

"I'm hot, Mommy." Three-year-old Logan pulled at her hand. "I wanna go home."

"Just wait a few minutes more and we'll get some ice cream." With three-year-old Logan's hand still firmly clenched in hers, Mary Karen struggled to pull the money out of the pocket of her jeans.

"Does Connor get ice cream, too?"

Though her twins were identical, and strangers often had trouble telling the two apart, Mary Karen had never had that problem. She could even tell by their voice which one was speaking.

"Why wouldn't Connor get ice cream, Cal?"

she asked as the bills slid from her pocket and she gave the money to the woman.

The older woman handed Mary Karen her change. "Those are two cute kiddos you have there."

"Two?" Mary Karen dropped the change into her purse. "I think all three of them are pretty cute."

"I only see two," the woman said before turning to her next customer.

Mary Karen glanced down. Where seconds before three little boys had stood, there was now only Caleb and Logan. Her heart rose to her throat.

"Where's your twin?" she demanded, her voice breaking. "Where's Connor?"

Caleb shrugged. "I dunno."

Mary Karen scanned the crowd. Logan pulled on her hand, trying to get loose but she held on tight. So many people. So many places for a five-year-old to hide. So easy for a child to be taken.…

"Connor," she called out over the crowd, hysteria edging her voice. "You come, right now."

"Is this the runaway you're looking for?"

Mary Karen whirled. Standing behind her was Travis, his firm hand on Connor's shoulder. Tears of relief filled her eyes.

"Travis, ohmigod, thank you. I owe you bigtime." She shifted her gaze to her son. She didn't know whether to hug him or give him a good scolding. "What were you thinking? Running off like that?"

"I saw Travis," Connor said, not at all apologetic. "I wanted to show him my face."

When they'd first arrived at the farmer's market, Mary Karen had coughed up two dollars each and let the boys have their faces painted.

While Caleb had simply wanted his face colored blue, Connor had chosen to be a dog. The band-booster mom had painted his angelic face white then added freckles, whiskers and a black nose.

"I thought at first he was going to bite me." Travis pretended to shudder. "But then he said my name, and I knew it was Connor."

Mary Karen swallowed a laugh when her son growled and pretended to snap at the doctor. This was serious stuff. Taking off by himself could have had disastrous consequences.

She fixed her gaze on her strongest-willed son. Though she hated playing Mean Mom, Mary Karen had three boys and only two hands. The children had to obey her. Soon, she'd have four to manage and control would be even more crucial.

"I told you to stay by my side," she said in a firm tone. "That means you. Stay. By. My side. Have I made myself clear?"

Connor lifted his chin. "I don't like to wait."

"Well, sometimes we have to do things we don't like." Mary Karen met her son's gaze.

"You will be going to bed an hour early for the next three nights for disobeying me."

"But I didn't do anything wrong," Connor protested.

"You ran off." In spite of her rising temper Mary Karen's voice remained calm. She'd learned long ago that if she lost control, the boys stopped listening. "You could have gotten lost. A stranger could have taken you. All sorts of bad things could have happened."

Connor's expression turned mulish. "But—"

"One more word and I'll make it two hours early," she warned.

"I'd listen to her, Con." Travis knew Connor was too young to fully appreciate the serious-ness of being a child alone in this crowd. But the boy needed to listen to his mother. Though Jackson was a safe town, crime happened here like anywhere else.

M.K. was a caring mother who wanted her children to be not only happy, but safe as well.

It suddenly hit him that his child would be lucky to have her watching over them. The thought— and the accompanying dip in his gut—took him by surprise. Travis shifted his gaze back to the mother of his unborn child.

He frowned. Mary Karen's cheeks were flushed and perspiration dotted her brow. Yet her eyes were clear and she didn't look feverish. He studied her for a few seconds longer and decided it had to be the layers of clothing. In addition to jeans and her favorite red long-sleeved tee, she wore a jacket heavy enough for winter.

"Give me your coat." He held out his hand to her. "You look warm."

Her gaze dropped to Connor and the jacket he'd tied around the boy's waist.

"I'm fine," she said. "But I think the boys may be hot."

"Tie mine like you did my brother's," Caleb said.

"Me, too," Logan echoed.

Travis released his hold on Connor's hand.

"Stay put," he ordered, before turning to the other two. He quickly secured their jackets around their waists while watching Mary Karen out of the corner of his eye. Travis knew she had to be hot, too. Although it was unzipped, was keeping on the coat her way of trying to cover up her pregnancy?

Guilt sluiced through him knowing it had been his unquenchable desire for her that had put her in this position. But he would make it right. He just needed to follow his plan and convince her that he'd changed his mind, that he really did want a family, after all.

"You know I came to the farmer's market looking for you," he told Mary Karen. "I was hoping to take you and the boys out to lunch."

He continued before the no had a chance to cross her lips. "A large pepperoni at Perfect Pizza? With something icy cold to drink?"

"I want pizza," Caleb said, and his two brothers nodded vigorously in agreement.

"C'mon, M.K.," he said in his most persuasive tone. "Doesn't a great big glass of iced tea sound good to you?"

Mary Karen wiped the perspiration from her face, the bag of vegetables dangling from her hand. "Okay."

The boys cheered. Travis wanted to cheer, too. Not because of the food, but because his plan to win her over had just taken a step forward.

And it had been his experience that every success began with a single step.

Chapter Six

Travis kept Mary Karen laughing on the short walk to the restaurant while the boys focused on making sure they stepped on every crack in the sidewalk. The popular eatery was filling up so while Travis got in line to order, Mary Karen commandeered a large booth in the corner of the room. Once she was in the booth, she slithered out of the jacket and immediately felt better.

She should have taken off the coat, but couldn't take the chance of someone noticing her rapidly expanding belly. Still, Mary Karen knew she couldn't go on hiding forever. One week more, maybe two. Then she'd come clean.

She pulled out the crayons she always kept in her purse and turned over the paper place mats for the boys to draw on. While they colored, she tugged down the front of her shirt and touched up her lip gloss. She'd just dropped the tube into her pocket when Travis walked up.

"It shouldn't be long." He smiled and slid in next to Connor, directly across from Mary Karen. His head cocked as he surveyed the table. "Where'd they get the crayons?"

Mary Karen gestured to the large bag at her feet. "They're a staple. I never go anywhere without them."

"You're amazing." The look of admiration in his eyes took her by surprise. "The boys are lucky to have you for a mother."

"I'm not so sure about that," Mary Karen said with a rueful smile.

She'd been only twenty-one when the twins had been born. Going from carefree college girl to mother of two had been a rough transition. She'd done her best but most days it felt as if she was merely treading water. "I'm a horrible cook. I clean but you certainly wouldn't want to eat off my floors and—"

"—you love your boys with your whole heart and put their welfare ahead of your own needs." Travis waved a dismissive hand. "That other stuff doesn't matter."

Mary Karen hugged the compliment close as unexpected emotion clogged her throat. She was spared from having to say anything by the waitress appearing with their drinks. Iced tea for her. Milk for Travis and her sons. When the boys wrinkled up their nose at the milk, Travis took a big, noisy sip of his. Before long they were drinking their milk noisily, too.

Travis was so good with children, it was a shame he didn't want any of his own. Of course, right now, the way he was teasing the boys and coloring alongside them, you'd never have known he'd been determined to be childless.

Mary Karen couldn't have said what they talked about until the pizza came, only that Travis did a good job of including the boys in the conversation. By the time they finished everyone was full and content.

"Thanks for the pizza, Trav," Mary Karen said when he refused her offer to pay. "You didn't have to buy."

Travis winked. "A gentleman never lets his date pay."

"But this isn't a date," she reminded him.

"You say to-ma-to," he said. "I say to-mah-to."

She rolled her eyes. "What am I going to do with you?"

"I've got some ideas." He wiggled his ears. It was a talent he'd honed during his middle school years. "None of them appropriate in present company."

Mary Karen chuckled. The ear thing should have turned her off. Instead it made her smile, just as it had when she'd been eight. The unexpected antic was so totally Travis.

He'd always had a special something that had drawn her to him. Call her crazy but she found his off-beat sense of humor very appealing.

Not to mention his boy-next-door brand of sex appeal. Today, that was out in full force. His sandy-colored hair, which normally looked as if he'd raked his hand through it, lay perfectly in a stylish razor cut. The long-sleeved green shirt she'd given him for Christmas brought out the emerald in his hazel eyes. It was no wonder she'd cast her good sense to the wind in Vegas and married him....

"Will you do it?"

Mary Karen blinked and pulled her thoughts back to the present. "Pardon me?"

"The hospital awards banquet is tonight," he said. "I'd like you to come with me as my guest."

Mary Karen had attended this event several times before. She knew the food would be superb, the atmosphere elegant and the mood a tad romantic...which was precisely why she shouldn't attend. Not with Travis. Too many potential landmines.

"Think of it as a chance to spend an evening having my undivided attention," he said, flashing that impudent Travis smile. "If that doesn't do it for you, think of it as a free meal or an excuse to dress up or whatever else will get you to say yes."

He was determined to change her mind, but that wasn't happening. "It's tempting but—"

"C'mon, M.K.," he said. "Be a sport and say yes."

"Don't you want to go with Travis, Mommy?" Caleb asked, looking up from his coloring.

"Yeah, Mommy." Travis leaned forward. "Don't you want to go with me?"

For a second she found herself drowning in the depths of those hazel eyes, until she forced her gaze away. "I appreciate the invitation but it's too late for me to get a babysitter."

"If you had one, would you go?"

She glanced at her sons who'd obviously grown bored with the conversation and were now attempting to turn the place mats into paper airplanes. "You know as well as I do that not just any sitter can handle the three of them."

"It'd have to be someone you trusted," Travis agreed. "If you had such a person or persons, would you go with me?"

Knowing there was no way she could get a sitter who met her qualifications this late on a Saturday, Mary Karen smiled. "Of course."

"Great." A look of relief crossed Travis's face. "Then, we're set."

"Uh, not so fast. You have to find the baby-sitter first."

"Boys," Travis announced. "Your grandma and grandpa will be coming over tonight."

"Cool," Caleb said, smashing the tip of his plane into Logan's arm and making him howl.

Connor smiled. "Grandpa always lets me stay up late."

"Your grandpa will do as I—what am I saying?" Mary Karen stopped herself. "My parents are playing cards with Ron and Carol Evans this evening."

"They *were* playing cards," Travis said, a smug smile on his lips. "Carol has the flu and had to cancel. Your parents are now available to babysit."

As always, Travis seemed so confident, so sure. But Mary Karen had spoken with her mother this morning, just before she and the boys had left to walk downtown. "How could you possibly know that?"

"I ran into them a few minutes before Connor found me."

"The fact that their plans fell through doesn't mean they want to babysit," Mary Karen said, shooting Logan a look that said he'd better stop fussing and disturbing other customers.

Her three-year-old reacted by punching Connor in the arm.

Mary Karen sighed. But before she could admonish him, Travis took her hand and began caressing her palm with his thumb. "I told your parents about the banquet and dance this evening."

She pulled her hand away before her eyes closed. "Stop that," she hissed.

"They were happy to hear you're going out. Even if it was with me," he said without missing a beat. "They'll be over at five-thirty."

No fair, Mary Karen wanted to protest. She didn't need Travis coming around and playing nice. She needed to stay strong. Do this alone. For her sons' sakes.

The boys still asked about their daddy, still wondered why he wasn't around. They loved Travis. If he became an even bigger part of their lives and then left, they'd be devastated.

"M.K." His voice broke through her thoughts. "I want you there. You're my best friend. That hasn't changed."

Mary Karen felt a momentary twinge of disappointment at the thought of only being his best friend and nothing more. Which didn't make sense. They *were* best friends. Through the years she'd been able to count on that one constant.

"Please come with me," he said, offering her a smile that made her heart flip-flop.

The thought of the night she faced if she decided to turn down his offer and stay home gave her pause. She'd get to make dinner, clean up and watch the most recent Transformer movie…

again. After that, baths and bedtime before collapsing exhausted into bed, then getting up tomorrow and doing it all over again.

"You said you owed me," he reminded her.

Though he wasn't playing fair, she *did* owe him. He'd brought her son safely back to her. And really, what was the big deal? What would it hurt to spend a night enjoying good food and adult conversation?

She sighed. "Pick me up at six."

The ballroom of the Spring Gulch Country Club reminded Mary Karen of a beautiful garden party. Huge urns of flowers surrounded the shiny, wooden dance floor. Crystal goblets and sterling silver flatware gleamed in the candlelight. Most of those in attendance, men in tuxedoes and women in gorgeous cocktail dresses, were people Mary Karen had known her entire life.

Knowing the event would be dressy she'd chosen a black silky jersey dress with a long luxe tie. She hoped the one bare shoulder and long tie would draw attention upward, away from her rapidly growing baby bump.

Mary Karen didn't mind if people thought she'd gained a little weight. She just didn't want them knowing she was pregnant. Not yet.

July had tactfully asserted she needed to face facts. Mary Karen smiled at the thought. Every day her changing body brought her pregnancy up close and personal. Still, she hoped to get through the emotional roller coaster of this first trimester before dealing with everyone's disappointment when they learned how stupid she'd been…again.

"You okay?"

Mary Karen shifted her gaze to Travis, surprised at the concern in his eyes.

"I'm not going to throw up all over your new Italian loafers, if that's what you're worried about." Mary Karen forced a chuckle.

"That's a relief." He shot her a wink and set a reassuring hand on the small of her back as they crossed the room.

A group of young doctors that Travis often partied with stood by the bar, laughing uproariously. He didn't spare them a second glance. "What sounds better to you? Dancing or mingling?"

A cocktail hour and dancing always preceded the dinner and awards. Though Mary Karen normally loved to talk, tonight she preferred to surrender her worries and sway in time to big band music.

Of course, she began to regret her choice the second her "husband" pressed her tightly against his tuxedo-clad body. They'd danced together many times but she couldn't remember him ever holding her so closely before. She fought against the emotions and the desire the nearness engendered. Travis hadn't held her this tightly since they'd made love their wedding night in Vegas.

The woodsy scent of his cologne teased her nostrils. Unlike the smells which sent her stomach reeling, this scent tantalized and beckoned her closer. Mary Karen laid her head against his broad chest and let the music seep into her soul. They danced silently for several minutes. "You smell wonderful."

"It's the cologne you gave me for my birthday." Travis pressed her more firmly against him. "Every time I wear it I think of you."

The popular scent had been an impulsive purchase at the big box store out on the highway. The college student clerk had told her that "girls love this scent on their guys." When Mary Karen had heard that she'd smiled, wondering which of Travis's many girlfriends would reap the benefits of her gift.

"Why did you invite *me* to come with you,

Trav?" She kept her tone low, her words soft and for his ears only.

"You're my wife," he said, executing a series of turns that left her breathless. "Even if you weren't, there isn't another woman I'd rather be with tonight than you."

His response took her by surprise. Then she laughed. "You're so full of it."

For a second he looked askance then he chuckled. "And you my dear, are such a skeptic."

"Realist."

"Skeptic." His breath tickled her ear and sent a shiver up her spine. "Think about it. When everyone gets together, who is always my date?"

There was no need for him to explain who "everyone" was—they both knew it was the tight-knit group of friends and family who socialized together on a regular basis.

"That's only because you didn't want any of your girlfriends to think you were getting serious." Mary Karen slid her fingers through the hair at the nape of his neck. He'd always worn his hair a little longer than her brother's other friends, but on him it worked. "And you enjoy giving me a hard time."

"Wrong." Travis maneuvered them to the edge of the dance floor where it wasn't so crowded. "You and I fit. I enjoy your company. We like the same music, find humor in the same jokes. I venture to say there's no one on this earth who knows me as well as you do."

Mary Karen couldn't dispute his words. A wave of sadness washed over her at the realization of how close they'd grown these past couple of years. She did know him. And it was that intimate knowledge of his aversion to children that confirmed her belief that marriage between them would never work.

She sighed, wondering why the truth that had led them to split up all those years ago, still held the power to hurt. But it was why, when she discovered she was pregnant, she'd known there would be no happily ever after for her.

"I heard that," he said.

She blinked rapidly, clearing her eyes of unwanted moisture. "Heard what?"

"The I-know-him-so-well-and-that's-not-a-good-thing sigh," he said, his tone teasing.

Mary Karen simply smiled. Travis didn't want a wife. He definitely didn't want children. They could rehash the whys all night and nothing would change.

"C'mon, the least you can do is deny it." He dipped her low, gazing into her eyes. "Stroke my ego. Tell me what a wonderful guy I am. Reassure me that any woman would be lucky to have me."

There was an undercurrent to his words that she didn't understand, but she ignored it and fell easily into the teasing mode that epitomized their normal conversation. "You're okay."

"Okay?" He sounded shocked and slightly wounded. "Okay isn't even average."

"We both know there is *nothing* average about you." Impulsively she molded her body against his.

The instantaneous combustion had her pulling back, even as heat seared her veins.

For a second an answering fire sparked in his eyes then vanished. "I hope my awesome body and bedroom skills aren't all you like about me."

Mary Karen had known Travis for as long as she could remember. He and her brother, David, had been childhood friends. Tonight he seemed different from the bold, brash prankster who'd always been there for her. There was a crack in the confident facade that she couldn't recall ever seeing before.

Had her pregnancy done this to him? Was he worried her perception of him had been altered by their time together in Vegas? Surely not. Surely he realized how much he still meant to her.

"In addition to being sexy as hell, you're a good guy. You're sweet and kind and honest. You've never lied to me and I can't tell you how much that means." The words flowed from her mouth uncensored. Mary Karen stepped from his arms, her body trembling at an unexpected realization.

She loved this man. Had loved him for years but until this very moment hadn't admitted it to herself. Of course, what did it matter? Steven had shown her that love wasn't enough. She cleared her throat and forced a bright smile. "Do you mind if we step outside for a moment? It's awfully stuffy in here."

"You don't fool me." He took her hand. "You're just tired of stroking my battered ego and will use any excuse to get away."

"You found me out." Mary Karen gave a gentle tug, trying unsuccessfully to extricate her fingers. Touching him right now, knowing that she was in love with him, was playing with fire.

He smiled and tightened his hold.

"I like holding hands," he said as they wove their way through the linen-clad tables to a wall of French doors leading out onto a large veranda. "I bet you didn't know that about me."

"Actually I don't believe I've ever seen you hold hands with any of your girlfriends." In fact, Mary Karen was practically positive she'd never seen such a sight. The tall, leggy ski-bunny types were always hanging on to his arm. But him holding their hand? No.

"I'm not talking about them." Travis released her hand and opened the door. "I'm talking about *you.* I like holding your hand."

Mary Karen wasn't sure how to respond, so she said nothing. There were several other couples out on the veranda. Mary Karen slowed her steps not far from them, but Travis took her arm and they didn't stop until they reached the far end, a remote spot shrouded in darkness, the only light coming from the stars.

The air had turned chilly, near freezing. Mary Karen shivered and wrapped her arms around herself.

"This is getting to be a habit." Travis removed his coat, wrapping it around her before pulling her close, waving aside her weak protests.

"I'm sorry," she said. "I should have known it would be cold out here."

Though the temperatures in Jackson Hole could reach seventies during the day, the night could still hit freezing temperatures.

His arms tightened around her. "Who's cold?"

Suddenly Mary Karen wasn't, either.

Chapter Seven

Mary Karen expected Travis to try to kiss her but instead he shifted his gaze and stared into the night sky.

"Every time I see a sky filled with stars, I think of my sister Margaret."

Mary Karen stilled. Travis rarely spoke of his siblings.

"The night of our parents' funeral she showed me two stars just to the side of the Big Dipper," he continued. "She swore she'd never seen them before. Then she said something that really surprised me. Meg insisted our parents put those stars in the sky so we'd know they were still watching over us."

Mary Karen could see why he'd been surprised. His oldest sister had always been the practical one in his family.

"Those two." Travis leaned close and pointed. "They're the ones."

His cheek was right beside hers. She only had to turn her face a millimeter or two and their lips would be together. Instead Mary Karen rested her head against his.

For several long heartbeats they stood at the rail, silently gazing into the star-filled sky. Not even when they'd made love had she felt so close to him. She told herself the strong connection was due to their longtime friendship and shared past, nothing more. It didn't have a thing to do with love.

"I adored your parents." She spoke into the silence, her voice as soft as his had been seconds earlier. "I loved your dad's deep belly laugh. Your mom's fabulous cooking. They'd both joke that I had internal radar. Somehow I always managed to stop over when the cinnamon rolls were ready to come out of the oven."

A slight smile lifted his lips.

With eight children—and two busy parents—Travis's home had hummed with delicious smells, laughter…and love. Then, without warning, it had all come to an abrupt end.

Mary Karen thought of her own parents. She couldn't imagine losing them both. Never having a chance to say goodbye or tell them how much she loved them. "You must miss them terribly."

"I've been thinking about them a lot lately, remembering what it was like to be part of a family." Travis spoke into the darkness, his eyes focused straight ahead. "I never realized how much I miss having a home."

Mary Karen pulled her brows together. Travis had always insisted that all he needed to be happy were the three b's—a bed, a BMW and a big-screen. She'd never heard him talk about wanting a *home.*

Before she could question the odd comment, one of the banquet organizers opened the doors and called everyone inside.

Travis placed his hands on her shoulders and turned her toward the door.

Mary Karen wished they could stay and talk some more. Their conversation felt unfinished, like they were just getting to the important part. But already, everyone, including Travis, was moving toward the door.

His face gave nothing away, but when she handed him his jacket she caught a glimpse of sadness in his eyes. Though she'd told herself when she'd left her house that she'd keep her distance, just before they stepped inside, Mary Karen impulsively reached for his hand.

A spark flared in his hazel depths and his fingers tightened around hers, the sadness replaced by something more intense. Her heart pounded against her ribs and moistened her lips with the tip of her tongue.

"Everyone please take your seats." The voice of Harlan Stromberg, the CEO of the Jackson Hole Hospital filled the large ballroom.

Although most of the attendees began moving toward the tables, Travis strolled through the crowd, holding her hand tightly, stopping to speak to colleagues, introducing her to those she hadn't met before. There was a certain possessiveness to his tone that she hadn't heard before and a warmth in his eyes whenever his gaze fell on her.

Mary Karen was feeling a little possessive herself. Especially when they were approached by several women he'd dated. But while Travis was friendly enough, he also made it clear the only woman he was interested in tonight was the one at his side.

By the time the CEO ordered the crowd to be seated there were very few open spots. Mary Karen would have preferred a table closer to the back—in case a fast break to the restroom became necessary—but Travis led her to a table directly in front of the podium. It wasn't until they sat down that she noticed the reserved sign.

"Travis." She tugged on his sleeve, keeping her voice low. "This table is reserved."

The words had barely left her mouth when Harlan and Dr. Grant, the Chief Medical Officer, and their wives sat down. Mary Karen started to rise but Travis put a hand on her knee, keeping her seated.

"It's a shame David and his lovely wife couldn't be with us tonight." Anita Stromberg smiled at Travis and Mary Karen. She glanced at the two empty places at the table. "We kept the seats open just in case."

Puzzled, Mary Karen shifted her gaze to Travis, hoping for an explanation.

"They wanted to be here," Travis assured the woman, his gaze lingering on Anita's large diamond-encrusted cat broach. "But July has been having contractions off and on all day, so they decided to stay home."

"Harlan tells me they're having another boy." The older woman smiled at Mary Karen. "Sounds like your new nephew will be making his debut very soon."

Mary Karen kicked Travis under the table and pasted a smile on her lips. She couldn't believe he'd known about the contractions and hadn't said a word. Somehow, she had the feeling that wasn't the only thing he hadn't told her. "July is due any day so tonight could definitely be the night."

As much as she knew that her sister-in-law was ready for this pregnancy to be over, Mary Karen hoped July wouldn't be heading to the hospital any time soon. Her parents planned to watch David and July's one-year-old son when the new baby came. If that event occurred tonight…

"I should make a quick call," Mary Karen murmured, glancing toward the exit.

"Oh, my dear, can't it wait?" Anita Stromberg appeared genuinely distressed. "Harlan is ready to begin handing out the awards. You'll want to be here for that."

Actually Mary Karen would happily miss the boring presentations, but the way the two couples were looking at her, leaving now would be practically un-American. And even though she didn't have to worry about hospital politics, Travis did.

"You're right," Mary Karen said. "I don't want to miss the ceremony."

Harlan had just taken the podium when Travis leaned close.

"If you need to leave," he mouthed, "I'll cover for you."

"I was just going to call and check on July," Mary Karen whispered back. "It can wait."

Harlan tapped on the microphone. Once the conversation quieted, he gazed over the crowd. "Our first award of the evening is the Humanitarian Award. This honor is given to the member of our community who exemplifies what it means to help the underserved through medicine. I'm pleased to announce that this year's recipient is…Dr. Travis Fisher."

The room erupted in applause.

Mary Karen gasped and whirled in her seat.

Travis grinned, accepting the congratulations of the others at the table, none of whom appeared at all surprised by the announcement. It appeared that the only one who hadn't known he was receiving the award was her.

She grabbed his lapels and leaned close, speaking softly so that no one could overhear. "You are so dead."

His smile widened.

Mary Karen released her hold and sat back, irritated that he'd kept such important news from her. When he tried to grab her hand beneath the linen tablecloth, she placed her hands out of reach on the table and focused on the CEO.

Harlan had clearly missed his calling. Goodbye hospital administration, hello public speaker. Give the man a microphone and he could ad lib all night.

Mary Karen listened while he regaled the audience with Travis's many accomplishments. Harlan extolled the young doctor's work on enhancing obstetrical and gynecologic services at the free clinic in Jackson, his medical mission trip to Cameroon and even tossed in Travis's role as an advocate for tort reform in the state of Wyoming. By the time Harlan finished, Mary Karen was properly impressed.

The night passed quickly after Travis gave his acceptance speech, with colleagues coming up after dinner to offer their congratulations. Kate even stopped by the table. She didn't seem surprised to see the two of them together. Mary Karen didn't know if that was a good or a bad thing.

It wasn't until the event concluded and they were in Travis's sports car that Mary Karen let the smile slip from her lips.

"You've got some explaining to do, mister." She pinned him with her gaze. "Why didn't you tell me you were getting the Humanitarian Award this evening?"

He slipped a key into the ignition then sat back. "The subject never came up."

Hurt mixed with Mary Karen's rising irritation. She and this incredibly intelligent man could talk for hours about everything from sports to medicine. They could make love for hours, exploring every inch of each other's bodies. He'd had plenty of time to mention he was receiving the most prestigious award the hospital gave out. But he hadn't said a word. Heck, even his recent new-car purchase had been a surprise.

"Getting the award is a big deal, Trav," Mary Karen said. "You could have told me they were giving it to you."

"Ah, M.K.," he said finally, "there are a lot of people in this community who give a whole lot more than I do."

Mary Karen blinked. Travis was known for many things, but humility had never been one of them.

"Who are you?" she recoiled in mock horror. "And what have you done with Travis Fisher?"

He laughed then sobered. "Thanks for coming with me tonight. Having you beside me sharing the moment—well, it meant a lot."

There it was again, that strange vibe that she couldn't decipher.

"Well, I'm glad I was there, too." She kept her tone matter-of-fact. "But if I couldn't have gone, I'm sure Kate or one of your other friends we spoke with tonight would have been happy to sit at the head table with you. Then they could have had the pleasure of listening to Anita give the blow-by-blow of Ms. Kitty's hernia surgery over dinner."

Despite the fact that everyone knew how passionate Anita Stromberg was about her prize-winning Persian, Travis didn't even smile.

"If you hadn't come, I'd have gone alone." He shifted to face her. "I don't want anyone but you."

Before Mary Karen knew what was happening, he pulled her into his arms and began kissing her. She could have just said no but she was too busy kissing him back. Those darned pregnancy hormones fueled an explosive passion that took even her by surprise.

Heat swept down her spine as his mouth molded to hers. His lips were firm and demanding, exciting yet familiar. An ache began deep in her belly. Mary Karen slid her fingers into his wavy hair and eagerly opened her mouth to his probing tongue.

When his hand slipped inside her dress and covered her breast, ache became need. Still, Mary Karen was able to keep her mounting passion under some control until his thumb scraped the tip of her nipple.

Waves of pleasure gripped her and she shattered in his arms.

"And that's how it's done," he said with a smug smile.

Breathing hard, Mary Karen settled in against his shoulder. "And that's the Travis I know."

He chuckled softly and continued to disperse kisses across her face, her lips and down her neck until the tinted windows were steamed up and the parking lot was empty. Though her heart still tap-danced against her ribs, Mary Karen finally grabbed control of her rioting emotions and pushed him back.

"You are amazing." Travis kissed her softly

then trailed a finger up her arm. "Come to my place. We can finish what we started."

A wave of need almost swamped her good sense. Mary Karen could already visualize what would happen if she went to his apartment. They'd barely be inside the front door when clothes would hit the floor. At that point she'd forget she had three little boys at home, not to mention parents who were undoubtedly exhausted by now.

Still, when Travis leaned forward and scattered a string of kisses down her neck, she was oh, so tempted to agree.

"No can do." Mary Karen resisted the urge to sigh when he lifted his head and sat back.

For a second he looked as if he might argue but then he started the engine and peeled out of the parking lot.

Travis wheeled the BMW down the long winding drive as if he were driving the streets of Monte Carlo. By the time he reached the highway Mary Karen leaned her head back and closed her eyes, leaving Travis alone with his thoughts.

It had been a strange evening. His goal had been to make M.K. believe that he'd changed, that he was now ready to embrace home and hearth. The trouble was that as the evening progressed it had become harder for him to say where the acting ended and reality began.

Talking about his parents had taken him by surprise. And that bit about wanting a home had come out of nowhere. Of course, when he'd seen the look in Mary Karen's eyes, he'd realized it had been pure genius…just the sort of thing to convince her he was sincere.

Even as he rejoiced that his plan appeared to be working, he hated deceiving her. Trust had always been at the base of their relationship. When Steven had been jerking her around and she'd grown suspicious of all men, he'd promised that *he'd* never lie to her.

The greater good.

He had to keep reminding himself that's what this was all about. Mary Karen needed him. She would never let him be a husband to her unless she believed he'd changed.

Mary Karen's stubbornness was one of the things he lo—er, liked most about her. She was strong and determined but vulnerable at the same time. He pulled the car to a stop at a light several blocks from her house. While waiting for it to change he cast a sideways glance.

Though they'd done a good job of heating up the car before they'd headed for Jackson, he'd given her his jacket for the drive. Sometime during the ride home she'd pulled it around her like a blanket and snuggled up to it.

Her blond hair that had been pulled back from her face with sparkling pins, now lay tousled around her face. His heart swelled with emotion. He was reminded suddenly of when they'd dated, how much he'd like her and how hard it had been to let her go.

It was funny to think that the thing that had pushed them apart back then—having children—was what had forced them together now.

The truck behind him honked. Travis glanced up then hit the gas. In less than a minute, he'd wheeled the Roadster to a stop in front of her house.

"Umm." Her eyelids fluttered open. She blinked several times then leisurely yawned, covering her mouth with one hand. "Where are we?"

"Home sweet home." He thought about teasing her about always going to sleep on him, but stopped himself just in time. She was pregnant and needed her rest. Instead he brushed the crisscross pattern on her cheek with his knuckles.

She leaned into the caress. "What time is it?"

He gestured with his head toward the readout on the dash.

Mary Karen gasped.

"Ohmigod." She fumbled with her safety belt. "I promised Mom and Dad I'd be home an hour ago."

Though she insisted it wasn't necessary, Travis walked her to the door. She attempted to send him away again when they reached the porch but he told her it would be rude for him to leave without at least saying hello to her parents.

He'd known Bob and Linda Wahl his entire life. Growing up, if he and David weren't at the Fisher house, they were at the Wahl's. Unlike his chaotic household, David's home had been a refuge, a place where he could relax and catch his breath.

Mary Karen pulled the house key from her evening bag, but the door swung open before she could insert it in the lock.

"Travis." The look of delight that spread across Linda's face reinforced he'd made the right decision. "I never expected you to see Mary Karen all the way to the door."

"I'm not surprised." Bob Wahl reached past his wife and clasped Travis's hand. "The boy is a gentleman."

In that second, Travis was reminded of another reason he'd liked hanging out at the Wahl house. David's dad had always made him feel as if he was special, someone who could be trusted.

Travis wondered what Bob would say when he found out he'd gotten Mary Karen pregnant. He wouldn't be pleased, that was certain. *Unless* Travis could convince him that Mary Karen's life would be better with him at her side.

"How were the children?" Mary Karen asked.

Travis couldn't believe she'd asked. Knowing her boys, any questions about their conduct was risky.

"The boys were good," Linda assured her daughter. The pretty, former schoolteacher had dark, wavy hair just like her son's and a friendly smile. Her khaki pants were stained with juice and there was a handprint on her yellow button-down shirt.

Travis could only conclude that to this doting grandmother "good" had an entirely different meaning than it did for the general population.

"We took them on a long walk to the park, so they should sleep well tonight." Grandpa Bob's sandy-colored hair was sprinkled liberally with gray, but his face had very few lines and his blue eyes were still bright and clear. His jeans and University of Wyoming sweatshirt appeared to have made it through the evening unscathed.

Of course, Travis knew Bob and Linda would just say stains—and any rips and tears—came with the territory. The two considered their grandchildren gifts from God. Travis didn't doubt for a minute that, had his parents lived, they would have felt the same way. They'd have been thrilled with Mary Karen's pregnancy. And maybe, had they lived, he'd have been thrilled, too.

"Thank you for watching them." Mary Karen gave her mom a quick hug. "I didn't need to go—"

"Yes, you did." Linda held her daughter at arm's length. "You're twenty-six. You deserve to enjoy yourself. So tell me all about it. Don't leave anything out."

"Well, we sat with Harlan and Anita Stromberg and Dr. and Mrs. Grant for dinner," Mary Karen said. "I heard all about the surgery Anita's cat recent underwent, so if you have any questions about feline hernia repair, I'm your woman."

"Good to know," Linda said.

Travis could tell by the woman's expression

she wasn't sure if her daughter was joking or not.

"And, Travis here," Mary Karen elbowed him in the side, "received the Humanitarian Award."

"Very impressive," Bob said, slapping Travis on the back. "Congratulations."

"All that sounds well and good." Linda's gaze searched her daughter's face. "But tell me what you did that was fun."

A flush traveled up Mary Karen's cheeks and Travis knew she had to be thinking of their after-hours party in the car. She certainly couldn't be thinking of Harlan's speech.

"We danced," Travis said. "The band was great. And Mary Karen didn't step on my toes too many times."

"Hey," she shot back. "I'm a good dancer."

"You're a great dancer," Travis said. "And you're a lovely, intelligent companion. Who could ask for more?"

Bob's eyes took on a curious gleam.

"It was just too bad David and July couldn't attend," Mary Karen said, filling the unexpected silence.

"I don't think July felt up to it, not with the baby due any day now." Linda's expression softened. "You remember what that's like, don't you, sweetie?"

Mary Karen nodded and Travis swore he saw her smile wobble.

"What's the latest on the baby watch?" Travis asked.

"Contractions are intermittent." Linda picked a piece of what looked like pizza cheese off her pants. "I hoped we'd have a chance to meet our new grandson this evening, but it looks like that isn't going to happen."

"You sound excited," Travis said. "I'd think after four grandchildren, welcoming another one into the world would be old hat."

"Oh, honey." Linda placed a hand on his sleeve. "I'm sure seeing babies born every day desensitizes you, but just wait until it's your own flesh and blood. There's no greater thrill."

Travis sensed Mary Karen's eyes on him. He smiled. "I'm sure you're right. Some day."

Linda's eyes brightened. "Don't wait too long—"

"Linda, the man needs to find a wife first," Bob interrupted. "Love, then marriage, *then* babies. Everything in its proper order."

Beside him, Travis felt Mary Karen tense. That hadn't been the way it had gone for her that first time. He knew she still felt guilty for putting the proverbial cart before the horse.

"That's the ideal." Travis placed a reassuring hand on Mary Karen's shoulder but kept his attention on her parents. "But I think we all agree that children, however and whenever they show up, are always a blessing."

Linda shot her husband a quelling glance before turning to her daughter. "Of course they are."

"Speaking of your grandsons," Mary Karen said. "They'll be up with the roosters so I better be getting to bed."

"Sleep well, sweetheart." Linda gave her daughter another hug. "We'll see you at church."

"I'll pick you up at eight," Travis said to Mary Karen, earning startled looks from all three.

"You don't go to church." Mary Karen gave voice to what her parents were obviously thinking.

"I go," he said. "Just not that often. But I made it my New Year's resolution to attend regularly."

"It's June," Mary Karen reminded him.

"Never too late to work on a resolution." He shot her a wink. "Actually, why don't I stop by about seven-thirty and help you get the boys ready?"

"That's so nice of you, Travis." Linda smiled at her husband. "Isn't that sweet of him, Bob?"

Mary Karen's father nodded, but there was

a curiosity in his eyes that told Travis the man sensed something more was going on here.

"Are you sure?" Mary Karen asked as Travis headed to the door with her parents. "I mean you have to drive all the way home tonight then back over here in the morning. That's a lot of driving."

Travis paused, his hand on the doorknob. He cocked his head. "Are you suggesting I spend the night?"

Linda and Bob turned as one, their shocked gazes shifting from him to their daughter.

"Absolutely not," Mary Karen stammered.

"Travis, I hardly think that would be appropriate—" Linda began.

"I thought if Mary Karen was worried about time, I'd stay and sleep on the couch." He smiled brightly. "But you're right. Unless we're married, spending the night wouldn't be appropriate."

Mary Karen made a little choking sound, and

he knew if he was close enough he'd have gotten another kick to the shins. But this was part of his plan. Her parents needed to begin thinking of them as a couple. That way they wouldn't be so shocked when they heard he was already their son-in-law and the father of M.K.'s fourth child.

Chapter Eight

Mary Karen caught the look of surprise on her sister-in-law's face the second July walked into the church and saw Travis. Mary Karen wasn't sure if it was seeing him in church when it wasn't a holiday or seeing him sitting beside her. Moving over to make room for July and her brother, Mary Karen took Adam from David while he helped his wife get settled into the pew.

Adam squirmed in her arms, reaching out for his cousins.

"Let him go." July pushed her hair back from her face, looking exhausted although the day was only beginning. "David will grab him if he gets out of control."

Travis, who sat on Mary Karen's other side, lifted the boy from her arms. "I'll watch him."

Adam blinked solemnly at Travis, until Travis made a face that caused the child to squeal with delight and spit up all over the front of his new white shirt.

Travis glanced down. He opened his mouth then shut it.

Mary Karen's eyes widened.

Her brother smiled, tossed Travis a cloth diaper and took back his son.

"What's with you two?" July whispered in her ear. "Are you together?"

"No, no, no," Mary Karen whispered back. "Absolutely not."

She rose to her feet for the opening hymn,

while Travis remained sitting, scrubbing baby puke off the front of his expensive shirt.

The fact that Travis didn't complain told Mary Karen that he was up to something. If she had to hazard a guess she'd say he was trying to convince her that he wanted to be a family man. She knew better. She knew *him.*

Mary Karen knew she probably should have called Travis's cell after he left last night and told him not to bother coming this morning. Letting him attend church with her and the boys only gave him false hope that she would weaken and eventually give in. She couldn't. Mary Karen had to look out for what was best for her boys.

From the moment Connor and Caleb had made their appearance in this world, her children had become her priority. Their welfare always came first.

She'd tried to make her marriage work. Her father had been such a big part of her life that she'd wanted the same for her sons. But when Steven had decided he wanted out, there had been no changing his mind. Before he left he'd confessed he never wanted to marry her. In fact, he said he'd been planning to break up with her the day she'd announced she was pregnant.

Mary Karen clenched her teeth. So she hadn't been what he'd wanted. He hadn't exactly been her Prince Charming, either. She shoved the bad memories aside and sang with extra fervor.

The sermon followed the second hymn. Mary Karen caught sight of her parents sitting near the front with their Bible study group. She gave her mom a little wave, feeling surprisingly re-laxed.

With Travis keeping the boys under control, Mary Karen was able to listen without her attention being pulled in three different directions.

By the time church was over, Travis looked a little frazzled. But he immediately accepted

David's invitation to breakfast at The Coffee Pot while the boys were in Sunday School.

Mary Karen stopped beside her ten-year-old minivan and held out the keys. "Want to drive?"

His BMW had been left at her house. They'd had no choice but to take her vehicle to church because a two-seater didn't cut it for two adults and three children.

"Go ahead." Travis opened the driver's side door for her and grinned. "Ethel likes you better than me."

When the blue van had first come off the showroom floor, Mary Karen's father had christened her "Ethel" because of the resemblance to a certain blue-haired, great-aunt in Ohio. The name had stuck.

Then, when Mary Karen had announced she was pregnant with Logan, her dad had given Ethel to her and Steven.

Her parents had known there would be no way they'd be able to get *three* car seats into their

Chevy sedan. Ethel had been a generous and much needed gift. Yet, in Mary Karen's mind, the van's arrival had also marked the beginning of the end of her marriage.

As Steven had walked around the vehicle, listening to her dad extol Ethel's many features, his resentful gaze had sought hers. Something had told her he didn't plan to be around long enough to worry about that third baby seat.

Carting around three children in a used minivan wasn't what Steven had envisioned when he'd graduated from college a few years earlier. According to him, his life was one big disappointment beginning with the day they'd said their vows.

His once perky sorority girl didn't want to go out and party with him. She wanted to take care of her twin babies and, when she did have some spare time, catch up on her sleep.

"Having trouble getting into the monster truck?" Travis's teasing voice jolted her back to the present. "If you need help, I'll be happy to give you a boost."

His hand cupped her backside, sparking all sorts of interesting thoughts, none of them appropriate for a church parking lot.

"I'm good." Ignoring the sensations, Mary Karen hopped into the van and hurriedly slid behind the steering wheel.

Travis chuckled and shut the door behind her. "Coward."

During the short drive to the downtown café, Mary Karen's thoughts kept returning to her failed marriage. She'd always taken responsibility for her part, but perhaps Steven was right. Maybe it *had* been all her fault.

By the time she found a parking space and they walked to the restaurant, even the bright skies overhead couldn't bolster her sagging mood.

They were almost to the door when Travis paused, his gaze surveying her slowly from head to toe. "I don't know if I mentioned it before but you look extra pretty today. Blue is definitely your color."

A spurt of pleasure shot through Mary Karen's veins. Her mother had told her the same thing when she'd purchased the dress on one of their rare shopping trips to the mall. "Thank you."

Travis continued to gaze appreciatively at the wraparound dress that showed just a hint of cleavage. "Yep, very pretty. You're obviously feeling better."

He took her arm and they stepped aside to let an older couple pass by them on the sidewalk.

"The nausea is pretty much gone," she admitted. "I'm not quite so tired."

"You're a strong woman, M.K.," he said. "I've always admired that about you."

Another compliment? Mary Karen wasn't quite sure what was going on but the somber mood, which had wrapped itself around her shoulders like a heavy shawl, slipped to the sidewalk to pool at her feet.

"What are you two doing out here?" David called out as he sauntered up with his son in his arms and his very pregnant wife beside him. "You should be inside getting us a table."

"I saw you parking," Travis said easily, moving to the door and opening it. "Decided we might as well enjoy the nice weather and wait for you."

He and David followed Mary Karen and July inside.

"Table for four and a highchair, please," David told the hostess.

"Are Lexi and Nick coming?" Mary Karen had seen the couple in church seated toward the front. But when she'd looked for them after the service, they'd disappeared.

"I called Lex on the way over here. Apparently Addie isn't feeling well," July said. "They skipped out during the final hymn."

Nine-year-old Addie had been born during Lexi's last year in graduate school. Lexi and Addie's father had never married and for a long time Lexi believed there would be no happily ever after for her. Then she'd met Nick and they fell in love. Now he was her husband and in less than a month they'd be welcoming a baby into their family.

Though happy for her friend, Mary Karen couldn't help being the teensiest bit jealous. Until her trip to Vegas, she'd still secretly hoped that someday a man would come into her life and sweep her off her feet. A man who'd love her sons as much as Nick loved Addie. A man who'd look at her like Nick looked at Lexi, or David looked at July.

Okay, so maybe she hadn't really believed it would happen, but she'd *hoped.* Now that dream was gone.

All because she couldn't keep her hands off

the man pulling out her chair. Mr. Right for sex. Mr. Wrong, Wrong, Wrong for marriage.

She'd barely sat down when July motioned to her. "Come with me to the bathroom."

A shiver of warning skittered up Mary Karen's spine, but she pushed back her chair and rose to her feet. She only hoped this down-the-hall jaunt had more to do with her sister-in-law's bladder than her desire to play Twenty Questions.

Keeping secrets had never been Mary Karen's style. She was used to talking out her concerns with friends and family. That's why she'd confided in July. She'd known her friend would understand. After all, July had been single when she'd gotten pregnant with Adam. But that didn't mean that Mary Karen wanted to talk about her "situation" this morning.

The bathroom was a single stall, a fact Mary Karen felt sure July had forgotten until her sister-in-law pulled her inside and locked the door.

"What are you doing?" Mary Karen resisted the sudden urge to giggle. She hadn't hung out in a restroom with a girlfriend since she'd been in her teens. "There's barely enough room for one much less—"

"Four?" July leaned back against the sink, her belly bearing a strong resemblance to Connor's basketball.

Mary Karen had been about to say "three" but July was right. Two babies. Two baby mamas.

"I heard you went with Travis to the awards ceremony last night." July's eyes sparkled with curiosity. "I also heard he wanted to spend the night."

"It wasn't like that at all," Mary Karen protested, then stopped. "Where did you hear all this anyway?"

"From your mother." July's lips lifted in an innocent smile. "Want to know what else she told me?"

Mary Karen pretended to shudder. "I'm afraid to ask."

"Linda thinks Travis is falling in love with you. And—"

"She did not say that," Mary Karen interrupted.

"Yes, she did." July nodded her head decisively. "She thinks there's definitely something different in the way Travis looks at you."

Mary Karen shoved down the hope the words had fueled, angry at July for bringing it up and even angrier at herself for wanting it to be true.

"Well, Mom is mistaken," Mary Karen said in a flat tone.

A knock sounded at the door. "Is someone in there?"

July blew out an exasperated breath. "Yes, someone is in here," she called out. "That's why the door is locked."

"We should let her in." Mary Karen started forward but July dashed in between her and the door, showing surprising speed and agility for a woman carrying an extra thirty pounds out front.

"Oh, no, you don't." July put her hands on her hips, her green eyes flashing. "You're not leaving this room until you tell me why I had to find out from my husband that you and Travis are married."

Mary Karen heard the hurt in her friend's voice, saw it on her face. It was now clear what had prompted this little private party in the restroom.

The reason she hadn't said anything to July, or any of her other close friends about her Vegas wedding, was simple. Knowing how strongly they believed in honoring marriage vows, she was afraid they'd encourage her to give Travis a chance.

"How did David find out?" she asked, buying herself a little more time.

"Travis told him," July said pointedly. "You on

the other hand, told me about the baby but not that you married the guy. Seems like a rather important fact to omit."

With a resigned sigh, Mary Karen put the seat down on the toilet and gestured for July to sit. Then she began to pace, or as much as one could pace in such a tiny room. "Getting pregnant was one thing. Marrying Travis—a man who has always made it very clear how he felt about being tied down—was plain stupid."

July raised a hand. "Yet, for all his talk about being against marriage, Travis willingly stood in front of a preacher and said his vows."

Since July seemed to expect an answer, Mary Karen settled for a nod. "Well, we'd had a couple drinks—"

"Was he drunk?"

"No." Mary Karen stopped pacing, but kept her face turned from her sister-in-law's probing gaze. "He wasn't."

When Mary Karen looked back on that night,

it was that part that still puzzled her. Why *had* Travis said those vows? In fact, he'd been the one who'd brought up getting married, not her.

"I think Linda is right." July brought a finger to her lips, her gaze turning thoughtful. "I think Travis does love you. And I think he wanted to marry you. Now he's scared. But he'll come around. He won't let you go through this pregnancy alone."

"It's not him," Mary Karen grudgingly admitted. "I'm the one who wants the divorce."

"Divorce?" July's voice rose. "How can you be talking divorce? You just got married."

Her sister-in-law's response was just as she'd expected. Still, Mary Karen was determined to make her see reason. To understand why staying married wasn't an option.

"Travis never wanted a family. You know that. I know that." Mary Karen resisted the urge to sigh. "Heck, there isn't a person in Jackson who doesn't know that."

"People change," July said softly. "They fall in love."

"Not him."

"Are you sure about that?" Her sister-in-law's tone turned serious. "Enough that you're willing to bet your future on it? Sure enough that you're going to walk away from your marriage vows without giving him a chance?"

"It's not just about me I'm thinking of, July. What about my boys?" Mary Karen thought about her conversation with Joel the night of Travis's welcome home party. "There's nothing worse than a child being in a home where a stepparent doesn't want them."

"Travis Fisher adores your boys," July reminded her. "He'd never do anything to hurt them."

"He's never said he loves me." The words burst from Mary Karen's lips before she could stop them. "Not once. Not even on our wedding day."

"Ah, now we're getting to the heart of the matter." July's gaze took on an understanding gleam and her expression softened. "I remember how I felt when I was unsure of David's feelings."

"I want a husband who loves me." Mary Karen blinked back tears. "Is that so wrong? I don't want to spend the next fifty years with someone who only stayed with me out of duty."

"Are you sure Travis *doesn't* love you?"

"As a friend, yes. In the way you mean? I guess I don't know for sure...." Mary Karen felt a wave of despair mixed with a tiny bit of hope.

"If he told you he loved you, if he said the words, would you believe him?"

Mary Karen thought of all the years she'd known Travis, all the times he could have said what he knew she wanted to hear, but didn't. Still, by believing him she'd be putting her children's future happiness in his hands. Could she trust him to be honest with her?

"Yes," Mary Karen reluctantly admitted. "If he told me he loved me, I'd believe him."

"Good." With a groan, July pushed herself to a standing position. "Now you can get David in here."

Mary Karen cocked her head.

"My water broke." July pointed to a puddle at her feet. "Unless you want to do a restroom delivery, we'd better grab the guys and get to the hospital."

Chapter Nine

Travis glanced around the waiting room in the Jackson Hole hospital's newly redesigned birthing center. The furniture was comfortable, the pale green walls soothing and the flat screen television tuned to ESPN Sports. Still, it felt wrong to be out here with Mary Karen and Adam when he could be *in there.*

Unfortunately July had made it very clear that she didn't want a man she considered a friend anywhere near her while she was giving birth, even if he was the best OB in the region.

"You want to be with her, don't you?" Mary Karen spoke softly as if afraid she might waken her sleeping nephew. On the way to the hospital she'd called her parents and they'd agreed to pick up her boys from Sunday School so she could watch Adam for July and David.

"Duggan will take good care of July." Travis knew his partner was an excellent physician. That wasn't the issue. "It's just I like being in the center of the action, not on the sidelines."

Yet that's how he'd felt all through college, medical school and residency. Once his parents died and he'd taken on the responsibility of his siblings, everything had changed. He'd watched his friends doing what they wanted to do, when they wanted to do it, while he was stuck playing the role of the responsible adult. Now he was being forced back into that role again.

The door swung open and Travis jumped to his feet.

David strode into the room, a tiny blue bundle in his arms and a proud-papa grin on his lips. "Seven pounds, five ounces and a helluva set of lungs."

"How's July?" Mary Karen rose awkwardly, her sleeping nephew still in her arms.

"Doing great. She said this birth was much better than delivering in the E.R." David chuckled. "Can you believe that?"

"The quality of the attending doctor I'm sure made the difference," Travis deadpanned, knowing they were both recalling the day David had delivered his oldest son in the E.R.

"You're lucky I've got a baby in my arms, Fisher," David shot back.

"Speaking of my new nephew," Mary Karen stepped forward. "I'd like a closer look."

Travis took the still sleeping one-year-old from her arms and she moved to her brother's side.

David gently pushed back the blanket, showing off his new son.

"He's beautiful," she said, smiling up at her brother. "I'd forgotten how tiny they are when they're first born."

While Mary Karen inspected her nephew's fingers and toes, David met Travis's gaze. "Wait and see," he said softly. "There's no feeling on earth that compares to holding your own child in your arms for the first time."

Travis just smiled. His friend had made his feelings clear on the importance of home and family. While July and Mary Karen had been holding the ladies' room hostage, David had asked when Travis planned to move in with M.K. and be a real husband to her. His brother-in-law hadn't liked his answer.

The truth was Travis didn't know when Mary Karen would agree. But David was right about one thing, time was running out. M.K. was almost at the end of her first trimester and keeping her pregnancy a secret wouldn't be possible for much longer.

Which meant Travis had to move quickly. Because when the news broke that Mary Karen was pregnant again, he was determined to be by her side. Not just as the father of her baby, but as her husband.

Mary Karen's parents arrived at the hospital—with her three little boys in tow—less than thirty minutes after she'd called and told them about their new grandson.

Caleb stared through the glass partition for the longest time, then announced loudly that he wanted a baby brother.

His grandmother couldn't keep from chuckling. "You already have two brothers, Cal. Isn't that enough?"

Caleb crossed his arms and shook his head. "I want a *baby* brother," he said again.

Bob laughed. "Well, sport, I hate to disappoint you, but I don't see that happening. Your mommy keeps busy enough taking care of you and Connor and Logan."

Travis glanced at Mary Karen who was pretending to be engrossed in tying her youngest son's shoe.

"I don't know about that, Bob," Travis said. "Look at my family. My mom had eight kids."

"Your mother also had a husband," Bob pointed out.

"That's true." Travis ignored the warning look Mary Karen shot him. "I'm just saying that you never know when Mary Karen might find some terrific guy, fall in love, get married and have another baby."

"I guess anything is possible," Bob said with great reluctance.

When the boys started racing up and down the halls, Travis knew it was time to leave. The fact that Mary Karen didn't say much on the way to the car told him he was in trouble. The fact that she kept the conversation light all the way to her home told him he'd crossed a line.

The moment they stepped inside the house, Mary Karen sent the boys out to play in the backyard. Travis helped himself to a soda from the fridge.

For several long seconds M.K. watched the boys from the kitchen window while Travis sipped his cola and waited.

"What were you thinking?" she said finally. "Baiting my dad like that?"

"I was simply trying to get him thinking about the possibility of you marrying and having more children." Travis knew this was a difficult time for Mary Karen and he certainly hadn't meant to make it any harder. "Upsetting you wasn't my intention at all."

He wrapped his arms around her waist and pulled her tightly against him. When she slipped her arms around his shoulders and rested her head against his neck, he let out the breath he didn't even know he'd been holding.

He breathed in the clean, fresh scent of her and let himself relax. This closeness was something he'd never experienced with anyone else but her. Mary Karen understood him. She accepted him, faults and all. He couldn't imagine what it would be like not having her in his life. "Have you ever thought about the fact that all actions have consequences?"

She jerked her head up. "If you're talking about my hopping into bed with you and ending up pregnant, the answer is yes. I'm well aware actions have consequences."

"Actually I was referring to myself."

A look of puzzlement crossed her face.

"I've finally come to realize that living my life the way I've been, has prevented me from having the life that I really want, with you and the boys."

She stiffened in his arms. "What are you saying?"

He stepped back and took her hands. "I'm saying that I want to be a part of your life. I want to be a part of our child's life. I want that very much."

Travis met her searching gaze unflinchingly, willing her to see his sincerity. He couldn't bear the thought of her going through this alone.

"My doctor's appointment is tomorrow at two." She lifted a shoulder in a shrug. "You can come with me...if it works for your schedule."

Relief washed over him. He brought her fingers to his lips and kissed each one. "I'll make it work."

"Cool." She snatched her hand back and pushed him toward the door. "Now, it's time for you to leave. I have a lot of work to do and I'm not going to get it done with you distracting me."

Travis had been kicked out of her house too

many times in the past to take this one personally. All that mattered was she'd agreed to let him go to her doctor's appointment with her. It was another step forward. And, for now, any movement in the right direction would have to be good enough.

"Any second now and we should see your little one," Dr. Michelle Kerns said with a warm smile as the radiology tech slid the ultrasound transducer across Mary Karen's belly.

Travis had only met Dr. Kerns a couple of times before. Today had solidified his initial impression that she had the kind of personality that would make Mary Karen feel at ease. So far everything had gone well, save a minor incident when they'd first checked in.

When the receptionist had called Mary Karen "Mrs. Vaughn" he'd quietly clarified her last name was "Fisher" now. Mary Karen had opened her mouth as if she'd wanted to say something then shut it without speaking. Perhaps it was because the waiting room had been full and she hadn't wanted to make a scene. He hoped it was because she understood that he didn't want his wife or baby carrying her ex-husband's name.

"Oh, my." The tech gave a nervous giggle.

Travis focused on the screen. His heart did a flip-flop in his chest. Dr. Kerns met his gaze, a tiny smile playing at the corners of her lips.

Mary Karen's eyes moved from the small screen to his face, and he could tell she'd picked up on the strange vibes in the room. "What's wrong?"

"Everything looks good, Mrs. Fisher." Dr. Kerns placed a reassuring hand on Mary Karen's arm then glanced at Travis. "Do you want to tell your wife the news or shall I?"

Travis forced a smile to his suddenly frozen lips. "I'd like to tell her myself," he said. "If we could have a couple minutes of privacy..."

The doctor and the radiology technician exchanged puzzled glances but obligingly filed out of the small room, pulling the door shut behind them.

Mary Karen pushed up, her elbows resting on the exam table, her eyes dark with concern. "Something is wrong. I know it."

"Nothing's wrong. You heard Dr. Kerns." Travis knew he should just come out and tell her but he hesitated, trying to think of some way to soften the blow.

"Why else would you want to talk to me alone?" she demanded, her worry turning to anger. "Tell me, Travis. What's wrong with our baby?"

Her eyes were full of fear, but there was strength in the blue depths. Regret rose to his throat. If only she didn't have to face this challenge again. If only they'd used a condom…

"Trav?" Her voice broke and when a tear slipped down her cheek he knew he couldn't put off telling her any longer.

He took her hand, squeezing her fingers tight. "M.K., you and me, we're not just having one baby. We're having two."

With twins in her side of the family and in his, he couldn't believe he'd never considered the possibility.

"No." The word came out on a deep moan. Her body began to tremble. "No. Not again. There must be some mistake."

He pulled her close, ignoring her protests. "Two heartbeats don't lie."

"I can't do this again, Trav," she whispered against his chest, her tears dampening the front of his shirt.

"Ah, M.K." Travis thought of the hearts he'd seen beating and a protective surge of emotion rushed through him. He hadn't been ready for one baby, much less two, but they'd make this work. Somehow. Some way.

"It will be okay," he vowed.

"You don't know what it's like to care for

two babies at once." Mary Karen drew a shaky breath. "You have no idea."

"But this time you'll have me. I'll be there for you and our babies," he said, his heart clenching at the pain in her voice. "I love you, Mary Karen."

She lifted her head, tiny beads of moisture clinging to her lashes, her eyes wide.

His words surprised him as much as they did her.

"You—you love me?"

Travis stared into the tear-streaked face of the woman he'd known his entire life. A woman he admired. A woman who could always make him laugh. A woman who was his wife and the mother of his baby, er, babies.

If the emotion welling up inside him wasn't love, it was pretty darn close.

"I do." With gentle fingers, he tipped her chin up and brushed a soft kiss across her lips. "And I will take good care of you and our children."

He wasn't sure what he'd expected but when she flung her arms around his neck, for that moment all was right in his world.

"I love you, too." The words tumbled from her lips as if they'd been poised there, waiting for just the right moment. "It took me a while to realize it, but once I did, I realized I'd loved you since I was sixteen and I forced you to kiss me in my backyard. Remember?"

Travis smiled. How could he forget? He'd been twenty-two and in his first year of medical school. She'd been a junior in high school and determined that he should be the one to give her that all important first kiss.

"I thought you were kidding when you approached me," he said. "I couldn't imagine how such a pretty girl had made it all the way to sixteen without being kissed."

"I wanted it to be you." Her hand rose to cup his cheek. "Even back then you were the only one for me."

A knock sounded at the door.

"Is everything okay?" Dr. Kerns stuck her head inside.

Travis looked at his wife and smiled. "Everything is just fine. In fact, it couldn't be better."

By the time Travis dropped Mary Karen off in front of the house and sped off to the hospital in response to an urgent page, some of the euphoria over his declaration of love had started to fade and the reality of the daunting task of raising another set of twins hit her.

When Connor and Caleb came running to the door to greet her and her mother appeared with Logan in hand, looking more than a little frazzled, Mary Karen wanted to fall into her mother's arms and cry.

But she didn't. Like it or not, she was an adult. She only hoped that Pastor Schmidt had spoken the truth last week in church when he'd said that God never gives us more than we can handle.

Because from where she stood, she felt pretty overwhelmed. Thankfully her three boys were getting older and more self-sufficient.

"Mommy, Logan peed his pants like a widdle baby," Connor said in a taunting tone.

"I did not," Logan yelled back.

"He did, too," Caleb said.

Mary Karen held up a hand. So much for self-sufficient. She smiled at her youngest. "Everyone has an accident every now and then. It's no big deal."

"I took care of it," her mother said in a matter-of-fact tone. "Logan was simply having too much fun playing and didn't think about going potty until it was too late. Next time he'll remember."

Mary Karen smiled reassuringly at her youngest son. "Of course he will."

"We were just having lunch," Linda said. "Did you have a chance to eat after your doctor's appointment? If not, there's plenty left."

Her mother had assumed this was simply Mary Karen's yearly exam. Little did she know that today's visit was anything but routine.

"I'm fine," Mary Karen said. She'd eat later, for the babies' sake, but right now her stomach felt too unsettled.

"Boys," her mother ordered as the twins began shoving each other. "Back to the table and finish your lunch."

"Me and Caleb want to go to the park this afternoon." Connor glanced at his twin who nodded agreement. "Please, Mommy, please can we go to the park?"

Mary Karen thought of the piles of laundry that needed to be washed and the clothes in the mending basket awaiting her attention. Still, the sun shone bright and there might soon come a day when she felt too big and too bulky to make the jaunt to the park. "After you eat your lunch and help me clean up, then we'll go to the park."

They cheered so loudly her mother covered her ears.

"Shush." Mary Karen gestured toward the kitchen. "The sooner you finish your lunch, the sooner we can go to the park."

Connor started galloping down the hall but Caleb paused, holding out his hand. "You come, too."

Mary Karen planted a kiss on his blond curls. "I'll be there in a minute. I need to speak with Grandma about a couple of things first."

"C'mon, Cal." Connor returned to grab his brother's arm. "Race you to the table."

"I race, too." Logan pulled his hand from his grandma's and ran after his brothers.

By the time Mary Karen called out for them to slow down, they were out of sight.

Linda shook her head. "I don't know how you do it every day. Those boys have so much energy. Why I thought I was busy when I had you and your brother both at home. Two is one thing. Three is a whole different story."

If her mother felt that way about three, what would she think of five little ones? On the drive home Travis had told her he wanted to be with her when she told her parents about their marriage and the babies. But Mary Karen knew her mother, knew she'd get a more honest reaction if Travis wasn't in the room. "Mom, I know you need to get over to July and David's but I was wondering if you had a moment to talk?"

Although she'd tried to keep her tone matter-of-fact, something in her voice must have sounded slightly ominous because her mother stilled, the smile slipping from her lips. "Of course, honey. I always have time for you."

Mary Karen stepped out onto the porch and gestured with a hand toward the swing. "This will only take a few minutes. I promise."

Her mother hesitated, her worried gaze darting in the direction of the kitchen.

"Is the stove off? No pots and pans out that they could pull over? Knives out of reach?"

"Of course." Linda looked affronted that she would even ask.

"Then we should be okay," Mary Karen said. "This will take two minutes max."

They moved to the swing and once they'd sat down, her mother turned to face her. "What's going on?"

Mary Karen took a breath. And then another. She'd always tried to make her parents proud but so often had fallen short. She knew they'd been disappointed when she'd gotten pregnant her senior year in college. And Steven, well, the arrogant rich boy hadn't been the kind of man they'd wanted for a son-in-law. Still, they'd done their best to welcome him into the family.

They liked Travis. Genuinely liked him. But would they be happy to find he was now part of the family? And what would they think about the babies?

Mary Karen twisted her hands nervously in her lap, struggling to find the right words.

"Sweetheart, please tell me what's troubling you." Her mother's eyes were filled with concern. "Whatever it is, you know Daddy and I are here for you."

Mary Karen squared her shoulders. "It's not bad news. In fact, it's good."

The frown worrying Linda Wahl's brow disappeared. "I like good news."

"Remember when I went to Las Vegas this spring?"

"Of course I do. I couldn't imagine why you wanted to go alone, but you certainly came back refreshed." Her mother cocked her head. "Does your good news have something to do with the trip?"

"Actually it does." Mary Karen licked her suddenly dry lips. "When I was in Vegas I ran into Travis."

"Our Travis? But wasn't he in Africa?"

"He'd been at a medical convention in California and stopped off in Vegas before heading to Cameroon." Mary Karen took another deep breath and continued. "We ran into each other by the pool and he asked me to dinner."

"What an unexpected surprise," her mom said. "But how does this tie into your news?"

"I married him."

"Who?"

"Travis."

"I—I'm afraid I don't understand."

"Travis and I got married in Las Vegas."

"I'm sorry, honey. This isn't making any sense." Linda's gaze met hers. "You've been back from that trip for three months. You never said a word to me about getting married."

Mary Karen understood her mom's confusion. "That's because after Travis got back from Cameroon, we were planning on getting the marriage annulled."

"I take it those plans have changed?" her

mother asked cautiously as if trying to pick her way through an unfamiliar territory fraught with land mines.

"Yes. We're staying married." Mary Karen smiled. When Travis had told her he loved her, a giant weight had fallen from her shoulders. With love between them, they could handle any of life's challenges, including five children under the age of six.

"Why honey, that's wonderful." Her mother's quick smile warmed Mary Karen's heart. "Travis is a fine young man. You know your dad has always thought of him as a second son."

Mary Karen gave into the joy bubbling up inside her. "I hoped you'd be pleased."

"There's only one concern I have—" her mother began then stopped. "No it's none of my—"

"What is it, Mom?"

"It's his views on children," her mother said apologetically. "He's made it clear on many occasions how he feels about raising children. And you have three."

"I don't need a reminder, mother. I'm well aware how many children I have," Mary Karen said, her tone sharper than she'd intended.

"Of course you are."

"People change." Mary Karen lifted her chin, daring her mother to disagree. "Travis wants to be a father to my boys…and to the babies I'm carrying."

"I'm sure he—" Linda paused. "What did you say?"

"I got pregnant in Vegas on our wedding night." Though her cheeks burned Mary Karen somehow managed to keep her tone casual and offhand. "We found out today that we're having twins."

Chapter Ten

Travis clicked off his phone and swallowed a groan. According to the message she'd left, Mary Karen had told her mother everything, about the marriage, about the babies. Supposedly it had gone well.

Even though they'd agreed to wait and tell her parents together, he didn't blame her for confiding in her mother. Still, it put him in an awkward position with her father.

Bob Wahl was a straight shooter. A man who called things as he saw 'em. A man who believed in being honest and aboveboard in both his professional and personal life.

If he arrived home after work tonight and was given such news secondhand, Travis knew he'd drop a few notches in Bob's estimation.

Which meant Travis had to get to his father-in-law first.

He caught a break when he called from the hospital and learned that Bob was tied up with clients all afternoon and wasn't expected back in the office until five. This meant Travis still had a chance to catch him before he headed home. Although Linda could tell Bob the news over the phone, Travis had the feeling this was something she'd prefer to tell her husband in person.

After seeing his afternoon patients, Travis hopped into his car for the short drive to Teton Village. The sun shone brightly overhead, the temperature a comfortable seventy-four. Though he had time to change, Travis kept on the navy pants and plaid cotton shirt he'd worn to the office. Boots and jeans didn't seem appropriate for such an important meeting.

He arrived at the Property Management office of Teton Village at a quarter till five. A half hour later he was still waiting.

"He was supposed to be back by now," Bob's administrative assistant said with an apologetic smile. "I could leave a message for him to call you?"

"I'm fine waiting here alone, Jessy," Travis said. Although he and the leggy blonde had never dated, they had talked a couple of times over beers at Wally's Place, a local bar popular with the singles crowd. "If you need to get going, I can stay until Mr. Wahl gets back and make sure we lock up on our way out."

"You sure you don't mind?" Jessy pulled her bag out of a desk drawer. "It's Monday Madness at Wally's and you know how crazy it gets."

"You're right. If you want a seat, you'd better leave now." He smiled. "Good seeing you again."

"You, too." She hesitated at the door, her form-fitting blue dress leaving little to the imagination, her heels accentuating her long legs. "If you have time tonight, stop by the bar. It'd be fun to…talk."

Travis just smiled. He'd seen the gleam of interest in her eyes and knew that with very little encouragement, the night wouldn't stop with drinks. But even if he were still single, he'd never let it go that far. For the past couple of years, Mary Karen had been the only one in his bed.

It had been a good arrangement for both of them…until Vegas, when everything had gotten so out of hand. When he'd seen her in that little red bikini reading by the pool, he'd had to go over and say hello. He'd asked her to dinner and before dessert he'd proposed. For reasons he still didn't fully understand, marrying Mary Karen had seemed to make so much sense that night.

"Travis." Bob Wahl's deep voice pulled him from his reverie. "I saw Jessy on her way out and she told me you were waiting. What brings you out this way?"

"I was hoping you'd have a few minutes to talk," Travis said easily, rising to his feet.

"I always have time for you, son." Bob shook Travis's extended hand then took a seat in the burgundy leather chair opposite where Travis had been sitting. Once Travis had resumed his seat, Bob leaned forward. "What's on your mind? Must be important for you to come all the way out here."

Now that the time had come, Travis wasn't sure if being here without M.K. was a good idea. Still, he'd reached the point of no return. "I came to talk about Mary Karen."

A look of alarm skittered across the older man's face. "Is she okay?"

"She's fine," Travis reassured him. "She's home with the boys, planning a picnic lunch for tomorrow."

"That's right. Tomorrow's the fourth." Bob relaxed against the back of his chair. "It's hard to believe it's that time of year again."

Polite chitchat was fine but Travis knew that every minute he let this conversation deviate from its intended purpose only increased the chance that Linda would call. If she discovered her husband was with her new son-in-law, she just might spill the news over the phone.

"I've known Mary Karen a long time, Bob."

"Yes, yes you have. And you've been a good friend to her and to my grandsons."

"My feelings for your daughter go beyond friendship." Travis took a deep breath. "I realize it's customary for the man to ask the father's permission to marry, but we're a little past that point, so I'd appreciate your blessing."

"Of course I'll give you my blessing." Bob

paused as if finally realizing exactly what Travis had said. "I assume when you said you're beyond that point, that you've already asked my daughter to marry you and she said yes?"

"Actually." Travis met the man's gaze. "We're already married. We tied the knot in Vegas back in March."

"In March? You've been married to my daughter for three months." Bob straightened in his chair, his voice rising with each word, the tips of his ears now bright red. "Why is it that I'm just hearing about it now?"

"You realize neither of us are impulsive people." Travis chose his words carefully. "Despite our—our feelings for each other, we were shocked that we'd done something so impetuous. We planned on having the marriage annulled when I got back from Cameroon."

"But you didn't."

"No, the feelings were still there and we've been given an extra blessing."

Bob's brows pulled together. "What kind of blessing?"

"Mary Karen's pregnant. She conceived on our wedding night." Travis hoped his smile didn't appear forced. "We found out today that we're having twins."

"Twins!" Bob roared, springing to his feet. He opened his mouth then closed it. He crossed the room and slammed his palms against the window sill. "Not again."

The disappointment in Bob's tone filled the room, making Travis very glad that Mary Karen wasn't here.

"It's not the same at all." Travis rose to his feet. "Steven never loved your daughter. He never wanted to be a family man—"

"And you do?" Bob whirled. "I've heard you say a thousand times that your goal was to remain happily single and childless."

"That," Travis said with extra emphasis so there would be no misunderstanding, "was before. Before I realized how much your daughter meant to me. Before I saw my babies' heartbeats on that screen."

Travis crossed the room and stopped in front of Bob. He met the man's penetrating gaze with a steady one of his own. "I give you my word that I will do my best by Mary Karen and the children, all of them."

"You love her?"

Travis resisted the urge to look away. "Why else would I have married her?"

"But twins…do you have any idea what your facing?"

"I helped raise my seven younger siblings. Five should be a snap." Travis chuckled. "Especially with Mary Karen beside me. You raised a wonderful woman, Bob. She's a great mom, and I'm a lucky guy to have her as my wife. I know this all came as a shock—"

"What doesn't kill us makes us stronger," Bob muttered. His gaze searched Travis's face. "If you're not sincere, I want you to walk away now. I don't want you changing your mind like Steven did."

"No. No. I'm definitely sincere," Travis said. "I would never hurt Mary Karen or the children."

"Your word is good with me." Bob said with a satisfied nod and just like that the interrogation was over. He clapped a hand on Travis's shoulder. "Welcome to the family, son."

"Thanks, Bob."

"I have to say I'm happy to hear that Mary Karen loves you and you love her. She didn't have that with Steven and I know that broke her mother's heart."

Travis had the feeling it wasn't only Linda's heart that had been broken. Bob loved his daughter and seeing her stuck in a loveless match had hurt him, too.

It wouldn't be like that for him and Mary Karen, Travis vowed. He would do everything in his power to make her happy. To give her the type of life she deserved.

And, if that wasn't love, it would have to be enough.

"She didn't faint?" Travis dumped a handful of spaghetti into the boiling pan of water.

When he stopped by the house after speaking with her father, Mary Karen had greeted him with a kiss and invited him to dinner. Knowing the extent of her culinary skills, he hadn't expected much.

"Mom was shocked, no doubt about that." Mary Karen picked up a knife from the counter and began cutting the French bread into small slices. "But by the time she left, I think she was getting excited about the marriage and the babies."

"Your father came around, too," Travis said, omitting the part about Bob's reservations. "I think he was happy to have such a brilliant, talented and sexy guy be a part of his family."

Mary Karen rolled her eyes. "Yeah, I'm sure that was it."

Travis grinned and tossed a little salt into the boiling water. He'd never understood the purpose, but his sister Margaret used to do it every time she cooked spaghetti, so he figured it must be important.

"I think it was reassuring to them to know that we're in love.…"

"And that we're married." Travis put down the salt shaker down and leaned over to kiss her.

She surprised him by dropping the knife to the cutting board. Mary Karen slid her fingers through his hair, opening her mouth to his probing tongue.

"Mommy and Travis sittin' in a tree, K-I-S-S-I-N-G," Connor sang from the doorway.

Mary Karen tried to pull away but Travis held her tight.

"I like kissing your mom, Connor," Travis said in a matter-of-fact tone though he still felt slightly out of breath. "Remember what we talked about earlier?"

"You and Mommy are married," Connor said.

"And you're going to have a baby," Caleb said as he entered the room behind his twin. "An itty bitty baby brother."

Mary Karen shook her head. "We don't know that yet—"

"It's not just one baby, Cal," Connor interrupted. "Two babies. Mommy is having two babies. Like me 'n' you."

"Itty bitty baby," Logan repeated in a high-pitched tone. "I like babies."

"See," Travis whispered against her cheek. "I told you it would be okay."

"You're so smart," she said, happy to have been proven wrong.

She'd worried the boys might be angry or resentful, but they'd been more curious than anything else and thrilled that Travis would be moving in and be around all the time. They'd stopped over and told Lexi and Nick then called Rachel and Derek in California. So far everyone had been happy for them.

"Tomorrow, we'll start telling everyone," Travis said.

"I hope people aren't angry we kept this from them." Mary Karen thought of her hospital coworkers and some women from the church.

"They might be a little upset," Travis said, his arms still encircling her. "But they'll get over it when they see how happy we are."

"We are happy, aren't we, Travis? I mean, you don't have any regrets."

"The only regret I have," he said, kissing her neck, "is that I don't have you to myself right now."

"I promise." Mary Karen trailed a finger up his cheek and lowered her voice to a whisper.

"After the boys are in bed, you will have my full and undivided attention."

He smiled. "I'm going to hold you to that promise."

"I'm counting on it."

Chapter Eleven

After helping Mary Karen give the boys a bath, Travis sat on the sofa with a twin on each side and a three-year-old on his lap.

If the gang at Wally's could only see me now. His lips lifted in a wry smile.

Mary Karen placed the book she'd just read beside her in the chair and pulled out another from behind her back. "I have a special treat for you tonight, *The Terrible Troll-Bird.*"

The boys took one look at the mean-looking bird on the cover and brightened.

"I read that when I was a boy," Travis said. The memory brought with it a rush of warmth. He'd been about Connor and Caleb's age and there had been four—or was it five—children in his family by then? No matter how busy they'd been, his parents had always made time for stories. As they grew, older children took turns reading to the younger ones. "*The Terrible Troll-Bird* was one of my favorites."

"Mine, too," Mary Karen said.

They shared a smile and Travis realized with a jolt he didn't miss the bar and the darts and the music. At this moment, he was right where he wanted to be.

Mary Karen's blond hair shimmered like spun gold in the lamplight. Like the boys she was dressed for bed. Unlike their cartoon pj's she wore a silky blue nightie covered by an equally soft short robe.

At least Travis assumed it was soft. He hadn't yet gotten close enough to touch. But he vowed he would, before the night was out. It had been a long time since their night in Vegas.

"I want Travis to read it," Connor said.

"Please, Travis," Caleb echoed.

"I think you're elected." M.K. handed him the book with a flourish. "Logan, honey, why don't you come sit on my lap while he reads to us?"

"No." The three-year-old shook his head, his lower lip jutting out. "I stay here."

Travis glanced down at the boy and the twins on either side, fighting a rush of unexpected emotion. "He's okay where he is, M.K. Logan will make sure he sits back so the others can see the pictures."

The child responded by flinging himself back against Travis's T-shirt clad chest. Unlike everyone else in the room, Travis was still fully dressed. But the promise in Mary Karen's eyes told him that once they hit the bedroom, his clothes—and hers—would soon be on the floor.

But that wouldn't happen until the book was read and the children in bed.

Just as it had when he'd been seven, the story quickly drew Travis in. The children's eyes grew wider with each page.

"That bird is super mean," Caleb said.

"If the Troll-Bird tried to steal my horse," Connor's eyes blazed, "I'd shoot it, too."

Logan glanced at his mother, a frown worrying his brow. "I don't want the birdy to fly away with Blakken."

"It'll be okay." Travis shot the boy a reassuring smile then resumed reading. By the time he finished they were begging for another story. He glanced at Mary Karen.

She shook her head and leaned forward to pick up a book that had slipped to the floor, her robe gaping open to reveal an enticing amount of cleavage. "It's time for bed."

Travis hid a smile. He couldn't agree more.

"Your mother is right," he told the boys. "Tomorrow is going to be a big day."

Since Travis had been a small child, Independence Day had been his favorite holiday. Because it was the same every year he knew exactly how the day would go. The Jaycees would kick off the festivities with their annual pancake breakfast, followed by the Howdy Pardners' Fourth of July Parade and the Episcopal church's kids games. Then in the evening, "Music In the Hole," featuring the Grand Teton Music Festival Orchestra, would bring everyone in front of the outdoor stage at Alpine Field in west Jackson to enjoy patriotic music and a picnic dinner. The night would be capped off by fireworks at the base of Snow King Mountain.

This year, instead of simply enjoying the fireworks, Travis would experience all the events… with his new family. He found himself looking forward to tomorrow.

While the boys and their dog ran ahead down the hall, Travis followed, holding Mary Karen's hand. He couldn't believe what a difference a day made. Yesterday he'd been worried she might shut him out of her life forever. Now he'd never felt closer to her.

M.K. released his hand as they stepped inside the small room crowded with a set of bunk beds, a junior bed and three noisy boys.

Growing up, there wasn't a time Travis hadn't shared a room with a brother or two. There hadn't been money for a home big enough for everyone to have their own room. Well, Travis was going to make sure when their new home was built that each boy had his own room.

He found himself thinking of the house he and Mary Karen would build. Perhaps one at the base of the Tetons, near Nick and Lexi's home. M.K. would like living near friends. And he realized, so would he....

Travis made a mental note to ask Joel Dennes

to pull together some house plans for them to review next week.

"Time for prayers," Mary Karen said.

As if on cue, Henry, the cockapoo, obligingly jumped on the bed and rested his head on his paws. If that wasn't strange enough, the three rowdy little boys immediately dropped to their knees by Logan's bed.

He watched in stunned surprise as Logan and then Caleb went through a "thank you, God" list, ending with asking for blessings for everyone from Grandpa and Grandma to Henry.

When it came to Connor's turn, he slanted a look in Travis's direction before lowering his head. "Thank you for bringing us a daddy. Amen."

Swallowing past the sudden lump in his throat, Travis glanced at Mary Karen and found her blinking back tears.

"Okay, munchkins," she said, after clearing her throat. "Give me a hug."

One by one, the boys hugged their mother then surrounded Travis and hugged him, too. Like three little monkeys, the boys climbed into their beds. Travis tucked Logan in while M.K. did the same for Connor and Caleb.

He paused, unsure what came next. When Mary Karen headed for the door, he followed her.

She flipped off the light. "Good night, boys."

"Good night, Mommy," they called. "Good night, Daddy."

Travis exchanged a glance with Mary Karen in the darkened doorway while the boys dissolved in giggles.

M.K. pulled him out of the room and closed the door behind him. Two bright spots of pink colored her cheeks. "Sorry about that."

"Don't be," he said. "I'm flattered."

"Connor and Caleb hardly remember Steven. They were only two when he left." The smile that had been on Mary Karen's lips most of the night disappeared. "Logan has never even seen his dad."

Now that she mentioned it, Travis couldn't recall seeing Steven since he'd left town when Mary Karen had been pregnant with Logan. Yet, until this moment he hadn't realized that the jerk had abandoned his children so completely.

Travis clenched his jaw.

"David has done his best to fill in," Mary Karen said. "But an uncle isn't the same as having a father in the house."

"You're right," he said, remembering Uncle Len. "It isn't the same. Not at all."

Travis understood more than most how much having a dad around meant and the loss it could leave in a boy's heart when he was gone.

M.K. was treading carefully, knowing he hadn't been keen on having kids. Now he had two on the way and three who desperately needed a dad. Travis could no more walk away from them than he could have walked away from M.K. Or from his brothers and sisters all those years ago.

"You've got great kids," he said. "If they want to call me Daddy, that's okay with me."

"Really?" She turned, her eyes shining like sapphires in the hallway light. "You don't mind?"

"If Steven doesn't care—"

"Steven," Mary Karen snorted, "doesn't seem to recall that he has children. I doubt he remembers their names."

Travis reached past her and opened the bedroom door. He herded her inside her room—their room—then locked the door behind them. "That's his loss."

"Thank you, Travis." M.K. wrapped her arms around him resting her head against his neck. "I love you so much."

His heart somersaulted in his chest. He slid his hands up and down the sides of her body, breathing in the clean, fresh scent of her. She'd been his friend as long as he could remember. A friendship that had become "friends with benefits" six months after Logan's birth. Her divorce had been final and she'd been feeling lonely and down on herself.

Building his practice had left him with little free time. While Travis had dated off and on, he hadn't wanted any of those women to get the impression he was looking for anything serious. His unique relationship with Mary Karen had filled a void in both of their lives.

Now she was his wife.

"I can't imagine being married to anyone but you," he said, realizing it was true.

"That's sweet of you to say."

"Do you realize we can now make love anytime?" He untied the ribbons at the top of her robe and gently slipped it off her shoulders, letting it drop to her feet. "We can get naked and crazy like we did in Vegas—"

He reached for her nightie but she shook her head and took a step back.

"I don't have the body I had back then." Though her tone was light, he could see the uncertainty in her eyes. "I now have a baby bump the size of a large melon."

Not for the first time, Travis cursed Steven for his past comments, for his insensitivity, but most of all for making this beautiful desirable woman doubt her appeal.

Travis met her gaze, willing her to see the truth in his eyes. "Even when your belly looks like the Great Pumpkin, you'll still turn me on."

Mary Karen didn't want to doubt him but Steven's hurtful comments were seared into her soul.

"I was thinking that maybe—" she swallowed and forced a bright smile "—we could keep the lights off?"

She knew Travis had never been an in-the-dark kind of lover but the thought of being naked in the stark light made her tremble.

Travis gave her shoulder a comforting squeeze then moved to the window.

"What are you doing?" she asked, watching him adjust the blinds.

"You're right. Moonlight is much more romantic." After getting the wood slats so that the golden light streamed in while still maintaining privacy, Travis moved to the clock radio at her bedside. He fiddled with the controls until soft instrumental music filled the room. Then he turned and held out his hand.

"What do you have in mind?" Mary Karen didn't move a muscle and his hand slowly dropped to his side.

"I thought I'd give you a back rub," he said.

Without realizing what she was doing, Mary Karen dropped a hand to her bulging midsection, now covered by blue silk. "With my nightie on?"

"With. Or without," he said as if it didn't matter either way. "Your choice."

"A back rub sounds wonderful." Mary Karen propped pillows around her baby bump and stretched out on the bed. By the time he'd kneaded most of the knots from her shoulders, she was relaxed and warm. Very warm. "If you don't mind, I think I'll take this off."

His eyes glittered in the dim light but his smile gave nothing away. "Whatever makes you most comfortable."

M.K. slipped off the silky gown but when she lay down, she pulled the nightie up against the front of her.

If Travis noticed he gave no indication. He squeezed her shoulder reassuringly then began slow, sensual movements up and down her spine. Every now and then his fingers strayed, catching the curve of her breasts. It wasn't long until Mary Karen found herself wiggling, hoping to push his hand off course.

She was ready to demand he touch her breasts when he planted a kiss against the back of her neck and sat back.

"You're not stopping, are you?" she said, her voice filled with dismay.

"Nope." He grinned. "I'm simply finished with your back. Now it's time for the other side."

Mary Karen clutched the gown tightly to her chest. She knew she was being foolish but she couldn't stop the fear. If Travis berated her for being fat and left her alone in their bed…

"I'm not Steven, sweetheart. I won't hurt you like he did."

The words were so soft Mary Karen wondered if she'd only imagined them. She drew a shaky breath and sat up. Before she could say anything, Travis brought both hands to her face and kissed her. His mouth was soft and gentle, a warm caress, a reassurance of support and…love.

"Hoo-kay," she managed to say after the second slow kiss.

With great gentleness, he eased her back on the bed, lowering the silky gown to her waist before she realized what he was doing.

His hazel eyes darkened, looking like liquid chocolate in the light.

"You're so beautiful," he said in a husky voice that made her blood feel like warm honey sliding through her veins.

Suddenly he lifted her hand to his mouth and pressed a kiss in the palm, letting her feel the soft stroke of his tongue.

A smoldering heat flared, a sensation she no longer bothered to fight. This was Travis. Her best friend. Her husband. A man she could trust.

"It's getting warm in here," she murmured. "You have to be hot in those clothes. Perhaps you'd be more comfortable without them."

Mary Karen felt the last of her nervousness fade at his quick laughter. She certainly didn't have to ask twice. His clothes landed in a heap somewhere behind him.

Her gaze slid over him and her lips pursed with female appreciation. If she'd had any doubts whether her pregnant body turned him on, she had no doubts now.

Travis slid his hands up her arms, his stroking fingers sent shock waves of desire coursing through her body. Her nipples stiffened, straining toward the remembered delight of his touch.

Still, he continued to play nice, until she couldn't take it anymore. She captured his wrists then placed his hands on her breasts.

"Not moving fast enough for you, M.K.?" His words might be teasing but the look in his eyes told her he liked her boldness. Even as he asked, his fingers were giving her what she'd demanded.

His hand lifted and supported her yielding flesh as his thumbs brushed against the tight points of her nipples.

"Don't stop," Mary Karen groaned.

"Not on your life." He chuckled, a low pleasant rumbling sound as his mouth replaced his fingers. Travis took her left breast into his mouth, sucking and caressing with his tongue. Just when she thought she couldn't take any more, he moved to the other breast.

Mary Karen arched against him, tangling her hands in his hair. "Oh, God."

With a grin, Travis tossed the silk nightie to the floor and ran his tongue with maddening slowness from between her breasts to her belly.

He scattered kisses over her belly, while his hand slipped between her legs. Mary Karen shuddered and let her legs fall open.

"Please," she begged, dragging her hands through his thick wavy hair. "Please."

She didn't need to say more. Travis lifted his head then lowered himself between her legs, easing gently into the heat of her body.

"I don't want to hurt you," he said, the muscles in his shoulders and arms tight as he held himself above her.

"You won't." M.K. wrapped her fingers around the rock-hard muscles of his arms, swallowing a cry of pure pleasure as he began to move on her, within her, in a sensual rhythm as old as time.

She swept her legs around his hips and met him thrust for thrust until with a gasp she arched her back and came, faster than she'd wanted, his name on her lips when she shattered. A second later, Travis followed her over the edge with a low growl of completion.

For a long moment, only the sounds of their ragged breath filled the room. He eased himself from her only to settle by her side. Slowly his arm lifted to wrap around her, not confining, but comfortable.

"That was…nice," she said finally. Too late she realized *spectacular* had actually been the word she'd been searching for.

"It was…pleasurable," he said, looking as if he was trying not to smile.

"Since we have time, I think we should do it again." Mary Karen leaned over and slid her fingers across his washboard abs. "Only, you know, take it more slowly this time."

"Sounds like a plan." He chuckled and rolled her over on top of him, catching her mouth in a hard, deep kiss, practically giving her an orgasm right then and there.

Though she doubted she'd last any longer this time, M.K. was up for the challenge. And, glancing at Travis, he appeared up for it, too.

"I'll be right there," Mary Karen called out, pulling open the dresser drawer, curving her fingers around the soft velvet. She opened the box and placed the ring he'd purchased in Vegas on her left hand.

Family and close friends knew she and Travis

were married. Now it was time for the world to know.

Tomorrow he would move the rest of his stuff into her home and their life together would officially begin. She glanced down at the large emerald-cut yellow diamond. While she'd initially seen the ring as a symbol of her foolishness, she now saw it as a symbol of their love and their desire to make their marriage work.

She'd be lying if she said she wasn't scared. Scared that Travis would grow tired of her and the children and want his freedom, like Steven had. Scared that he didn't really love her—

Stop, she told herself. Travis had never lied to her. If he said he loved her, he did. Last night she'd not only seen the love in his eyes, she'd felt it in his touch. And, as far as the babies, the hint of moisture in his eyes when he'd looked at the screen and seen those two little heartbeats told the story.

"Mommy," Caleb said from the doorway.

"Daddy said all the pancakes are gonna be gone if we don't leave now."

"Daddy?"

The smile on Caleb's face disappeared, replaced by a wary expression. "Travis said we could call him that."

"That's okay. I didn't know the two of you had talked," Mary Karen reassured the worried child. "As far as running out of food, I've gone to the pancake breakfast since I was a little girl and they've never run out of food yet."

Caleb kicked at the hardwood floor with the tip of his sneaker. "I'm hungry."

"You know what, Cal? So am I." She'd awakened this morning with a voracious appetite.

Mary Karen cast one last look in the mirror. With the forecast of seventy-five and sunny, she'd grabbed jeans and an oversize T-shirt for the outing. But even the loose-fitting shirt couldn't hide her growing baby bump. The curse of having two pregnancies before this one.

"C'mon, Mommy." Caleb crossed the room and tugged at her hand. "This is going to be the funnest day ever."

"Yeah, Mommy." Travis appeared in the doorway, looking incredibly handsome in khaki pants and a green button-down shirt. "This is going to be the funnest day ever."

"I'm not your mommy." Mary Karen greeted him with a kiss.

"Thank God," he said against her mouth, kissing her back with such enthusiasm that she forget where she was until she heard Cal giggle.

"I'm going to tell Connor you're kissing again," the boy said then raced from the room.

Perhaps Mary Karen should have stepped from Travis's arms. But there was enough new bride in her that she nibbled on his ear instead.

He grinned and tightened his hold. "I enjoyed last night."

Her lips curved upward. "We never did take it slow."

"Going slow is highly overrated," he said, dipping his head and scattering kisses up her neck. "But I'm willing to try as many times as it takes to get it right."

His mouth closed over hers and Mary Karen let her eyes drift shut, losing herself in the closeness.

"See." Caleb's voice sounded from the doorway.

Mary Karen reluctantly opened her eyes. Caleb stood in the doorway with his two brothers.

"Told you they were kissing again," Caleb said.

"I like kissing my wife," Travis said and Mary Karen felt a flush of pleasure at the words.

"But we want pancakes," Logan said.

"Okay, buddy, we're going," Travis said, then shifted his gaze back to Mary Karen. "We'll take up where we left off later."

"You better believe it." Mary Karen found

herself humming when she left the room wondering how she'd gotten so lucky.

Not only did she have a best friend for a husband, he'd taken to fatherhood like a duck to water.

It almost seemed too good to be true....

No. Mary Karen stopped the thought before it could fully form.

Travis loved her.

She loved him.

She would not let any niggling doubts ruin what promised to be a very happy life together.

Chapter Twelve

It didn't take Travis long to realize that spending Independence Day with three children was very different than partying with a bunch of adults.

For starters, he never knew that eating a breakfast of eggs, sausage and pancakes could be so messy. Especially when the twins started a food fight and he found himself caught in the middle.

"Sorry about your shirt," Mary Karen said. The five of them had a great position on the sidewalk at the beginning of the parade route. "At least syrup will wash right out."

"No worries." Travis tugged at Logan's shoe which rested against his chest. "This covers it completely."

"I want to stay up here," Logan announced from his perch on Travis's shoulders.

Not counting the few seconds Logan tried to use his head as a bongo drum, Travis felt he'd gotten the easy assignment. Keeping track of one three-year-old was easy compared to M.K.'s duty. She had the daunting task of keeping two highly energetic twin boys under control.

Travis had offered to hold one of their hands, but she'd insisted that Logan would keep him busy enough.

Antique cars filled with area dignitaries passed by, delighting the boys with their odd-sounding horns. Travis had his eyes firmly on the road when the scent of a sultry perfume hit his nostrils.

"Travis?"

He turned slowly, making sure he kept a firm grip on Logan's legs. M.K. had been right again. The three-year-old was as slippery as a wiggly worm.

A tall woman in white linen pants with a pale yellow shirt stepped away from the crowd. "I was hoping our paths would cross."

Travis hadn't seen the beautiful brunette for several years. "Leila, this is a nice surprise. I thought you were living in Florida."

The dermatologist had only lasted one year in Jackson Hole. She'd complained about the cold and the snow to anyone who would listen. No one had been surprised she'd headed for a warmer climate.

"I'm still practicing in Pensacola," she said. "I'm just here visiting friends. I was going to call but I'd lost your cell number. I wanted to find out if the rumor I heard is true."

Travis offered her an easy smile. "And what rumor would that be?"

Her brown eyes twinkled. "That a certain handsome ob-gyn finally took the plunge and ordered a BMW Roadster."

Until this moment, Travis had forgotten about his and Leila's shared passion for sports cars.

"Z4, crimson red." Travis couldn't keep the satisfaction from his voice. "You'll have to see her. She's a beauty."

"An impractical car." Leila's lips tilted upward, reciting the comment they'd always gotten from others when they'd mentioned their dream cars. "Like my Jag XK convertible."

"You got the Jag?"

"Darn right I did." She nodded emphatically. "It was my first purchase when I moved to Florida."

"You realize it's totally impractical," he said in an exaggeratedly serious voice.

Leila grinned. "That only added to the car's appeal."

He shared a smile of understanding with Leila before her gaze lifted to the boy on his shoulders.

"And who is this fine young man?" she asked. "A nephew, perhaps?"

"I'm Logan," the boy shouted, then shoved several fingers in front of Travis's face. "I'm three."

For the first time, Leila appeared to notice Mary Karen, standing next to him. And Travis realized he'd forgotten his manners.

"Leila, I'd like you to meet my wife, Mary Karen," Travis said proudly. "M.K., this is Dr. Leila Otto. She was a dermatologist in Jackson for about a year before leaving us for sunny Florida."

Mary Karen smiled. "Dr. Otto. I think we may have met once at a hospital function."

"Please call me Leila." Leila returned Mary

Karen's smile. "You must be a special woman to get this one to settle down."

Leila chuckled. "I don't think I've ever dated anyone who was more determined than me to remain single."

"I just had to find the right woman." Travis shot Mary Karen a wink. "The funny thing was she'd been right under my nose all along."

"Look at the horses." Connor tugged on her hand.

"I want to ride in the wagon." Caleb hopped from one foot to the other. "Can I ride in the wagon next year?"

"I don't know, honey." Mary Karen smiled apologetically at Leila. "I'm talking to Travis's friend right now, so I need you not to interrupt."

"My goodness," Leila said, her gaze taking in the three young boys. "You two sure have your hands full today."

"We're going to have two more babies," Connor said loudly.

"Yeah," Caleb said. "Two more brothers."

"Or sisters," Mary Karen reminded him.

Leila met Travis's gaze, and he saw the shock in her eyes.

"Mary Karen and I are expecting twins at Christmastime," he explained.

Leila opened her mouth then closed it. Opened it again then began to laugh. "Ah, Travis, I'd forgotten what a jokester you can be. You almost had me believing you married a woman with three kids and are now having twins. Next you'll be telling me that you're selling the Roadster to buy a minivan."

Beside him, Travis felt Mary Karen stiffen. "Leila, I—"

"I bet you're either a sister or a sister-in-law," Leila said to Mary Karen. "Which is it?"

Travis glanced sideways. The color had left Mary Karen's face. For a woman who usually had plenty to say, she stood silent.

"It's no joke, Leila," Travis said firmly, meeting her gaze. "Mary Karen *is* my wife and we *are* having twins in December."

"I—I'm so sorry." Leila's cheeks turned bright red. "It's just the Travis I knew would never—" She stopped. "I'm sorry. I think I better stop before I dig myself any deeper."

"It was nice to see you again," Mary Karen said, but the smile had left her eyes.

"A group of us are planning to meet at Alpine Field to enjoy the concert. You two are welcome to join us." Leila's gaze settled on Logan who was pulling on Travis's hair. "Except no one has children so—"

"It's okay with me if you want to go with your friend." Mary Karen slanted him a sideways glance while struggling to hold on to Caleb and Connor.

"Thanks for the invitation Leila but my wife and I already have the entire day planned," Travis said before she could finish. "But, please be sure and tell everyone hello for me."

"If you change your mind…" Leila pulled a scrap of paper from her purse, wrote down a few numbers then pressed the paper into his hand. "That's my cell."

As Leila sauntered away, Mary Karen exhaled a breath. "I'm serious, Trav. If you want to spend time with your friends, don't let—"

"And I'm serious," Travis said, sounding shocked she'd even suggest he'd go. "The only people I want to spend time with today are you and the boys."

"Are you sure?"

"Sweetheart, trust me. I'm right where I want to be."

Travis sat with his new family at the base of Snow King Mountain and watched the fireworks light up the night sky over Jackson Hole. Mary Karen had placed a small radio beside them on the plaid blanket she'd pulled from the back of the van. Tuned to a local radio station, the patriotic music blaring into the night air had been synchronized to the fireworks show.

People from the community, many of whom Travis had known most of his life sat nearby, their blankets and lawn chairs covering the grassy slopes. They oohed and aahed in unison to the spectacular display. But it was the loud booms that seemed to shake the entire mountain that the children liked best.

"Woo-hoo," Connor cried out when an M-80-like explosion sounded again.

Caleb and Logan bounced up and down on the blanket and punched each other.

Travis slipped his arm around Mary Karen's shoulders and put his mouth close to her ear. "Does it mean I'm getting old if I say I could do with a little less noise?"

"I'm right there with you." She smiled, but the sparkle which had lit her eyes at breakfast had faded. Of course, it could simply be that she was tired. After all, they'd made love most of the night and had been busy all day.

Still, he knew Mary Karen, knew her so well he could tell by her tone of voice when she answered the phone how she was feeling. "What's wrong, honey?"

She raked her hair back with one hand and sighed. "Three children keep me hopping. How am I going to do it with five?"

"*You* aren't going to do anything. *We're* going to do it. And we'll do just fine."

"Your friend Leila looked at me like I was crazy."

"That's because one child would be too many for Leila." Travis had to admit that while it had been good to see his old friend, her jab about trading in his car for a minivan had left him with a bad taste in his mouth.

Come to think of it, when Leila had made the comment he'd seen something flare in Mary

Karen's eyes. Could that be what was on his wife's mind?

"Is this about my car?" Travis said in a low tone. "Are you wondering how we'll make it work with a minivan and a sports car?"

"I've thought about it, sure," Mary Karen admitted. "But it will be okay."

"But we'd be better off with another van or an SUV."

"Of course having another vehicle that everyone could ride in would be best but—"

"A man shouldn't have to give up everything, M.K.," Travis said with an intensity that surprised them both.

Her blue eyes flashed and she leaned forward pressing her hands into the blanket, shoving her face in front of his. "Let's get one thing straight. I didn't ask you to give up your precious car. I know better. I simply agreed with your comment that it would make more sense the other way. I also understand cars aren't always about making sense."

"Are you calling me irrational?"

"Oh, for goodness sake, grow up."

"Don't fight with him, Mommy," Caleb implored, his blue eyes filling with tears.

"Listen to him, Mommy," Connor said. "We don't want Travis to leave like Daddy did."

"I'm not going anywhere." Travis gave the boys a reassuring smile.

Mary Karen swiped at her eyes. "Travis and I aren't fighting, we're *discussing*."

"You used your mean voice," Logan pointed out.

"Enough," Travis said. "Your mom and I aren't arguing, and I'm not going anywhere. Now, let's enjoy the fireworks."

"Look." Mary Karen raised her hand and pointed. "That's a pretty one."

The boys lifted their eyes to the sky, to the bursts of glittering gold and silver stars followed by waterfalls of colors. Lost in his own thoughts, Travis barely noticed. As the show continued, all he could think about was the stricken look in Mary Karen's eyes when Connor had mentioned his father leaving.

He slipped an arm around her shoulders and leaned close. "I'm sorry. I don't know what got into me. Forgive me?"

Travis was prepared to grovel, but she accepted his apology with a simple nod and an "I'm sorry, too."

Something was amiss. How he'd acted was definitely a grievous offense.

Seconds later she touched his hand. "Would you mind terribly if we left now?"

The fireworks display was only half over and she'd told him earlier she was looking forward to the finale.

He searched her face. "Is something wrong?"

She tried to smile but ended up wincing instead. "My back is hurting."

A cold chill traveled up his spine, but he forced an offhand tone not wanting to alarm her. "How long has it been bothering you?"

She lifted a shoulder. "Off and on all day. But in the past fifteen minutes it's really started to ache."

Conscious of three sets of ears in close range, Travis lowered his voice, his entire attention focused on his wife. His pregnant wife. "Have you had any spotting?"

As he waited for her response, his heart began a tap dance against his ribs.

Even in the dim light, he could see her face pale. She placed a protective hand on her belly. "I—I don't think so. Do you think something is wrong with the babies?"

"I'm sure everything is fine," he said even as he began packing up their stuff. He motioned for the boys to help him. "It's been a long day," he told them. "I think it's best we leave now, beat the traffic."

Surprisingly the boys didn't argue. The five of them made their way to the van, fireworks still exploding in the overhead sky. But Travis's entire attention remained focused on the woman at his side. He knew the statistics, 10–25 percent of all clinically recognized pregnancies end in miscarriage. Most of those occur during the first thirteen weeks.

Mary Karen was at that thirteen-week mark. It was a good sign that they'd seen the heartbeats on the ultrasound, but even that didn't mean problems couldn't pop up.

Not counting last Sunday, it had been six months since Travis had been in a church. He couldn't remember the last time he'd asked God for anything.

But as he slid behind the wheel, he found himself praying…for his wife's well-being and for the safety of the two little lives she carried.

Instead of turning on the street leading to their home, Travis kept going straight.

"You missed the turn," Mary Karen said softly, trying not to wake the sleeping boys in the back.

"If it's okay with you, I thought we'd make a quick stop at the clinic."

"Did you forget something?"

Travis turned into the medical center's driveway and pulled to a stop behind the wood-and-stone structure. He kept his hands on the wheel, his gaze straight ahead. "I doubt either one of us will sleep until we know for sure everything is okay."

"What are you suggesting?"

"I'll do a quick check," Travis said with a reassuring smile. "Followed by an ultrasound."

Mary Karen turned in her seat and glanced in the back. Part of her wished she could simply head home, put the boys to bed and go to bed.

But she knew Travis was right. If they went home now, she'd worry all night.

"Shall we go inside?" he prompted.

Mary Karen nodded. "Boys," she said in a normal tone, "it's time to wake up."

Caleb rubbed his eyes then glanced out the window. "Where are we?"

"We're at the clinic. Travis and I have some uh, work to do. The good news is you get to play in the waiting room."

"Can we play with fishes?" Connor asked, a gleam in his eyes.

"You may watch but not touch them." Mary Karen looked from one boy to the next. "Understand? No putting your hands in the water."

Mary Karen still remembered the day she'd stopped by to drop off something for Travis. In a matter of seconds Connor had climbed onto a chair and "caught" a large Angel fish.

"No fishing," Travis said. "Understand?"

The boys looked at each other and nodded solemnly.

After getting the children settled in the waiting room, Mary Karen slipped to the back with Travis.

His meager attempt at light conversation didn't fool her. Over the years she'd learned that the tiny muscle along his jawline jumped when he was stressed. It was doing a good Mexican jumping bean imitation now.

The checkup and ultrasound went quickly and when Travis cracked a joke, Mary Karen relaxed.

"Looks good, M.K.," he said. "No signs of an impending miscarriage."

"Then why does my back hurt?" Mary Karen had done an OB rotation when she was getting her RN but that had been a long time ago. And her last two pregnancies had gone by without a hitch.

"A couple of explanations might fit." Travis took her hands. "But I think I'm to blame."

Mary Karen cocked her head.

"Stress," he said. "Caused by me."

At first she thought he was joking until she saw the guilt in his eyes.

"Oh, Trav," she said. "You make things easier for me. You don't stress me out."

"The car thing," he said. "I totally overreacted."

Mary Karen put her hand on his sleeve. "We *both* overreacted."

"It's just that I'd wanted that particular vehicle for so long and—"

"You don't have to explain it to me." While Mary Karen believed Travis loved her, she wasn't about to test that love on such an unimportant issue.

"So we're cool?"

Mary Karen smiled. God, how she loved this man. "We're cool."

He slipped his arms around her. "I had a good time today."

"Really? You wouldn't rather have been with Leila and the others?"

"Absolutely not," he murmured, kissing the edge of her mouth. "How 'bout we go home and I give you a back rub?"

Mary Karen raised her hands and rested them on his shoulders. "Just a back rub?"

"That will be totally up to you."

His lips closed over hers and the flame ignited. Passion flooded every part of Mary Karen's body, making her squirm to get closer.

When he stroked her lower lip with his tongue, she parted for him, eagerly anticipating his more intimate kiss.

"See, Cal, I told you they're not mad at each other." Connor's tone was filled with satisfaction.

"How do you know?" Logan asked.

"Cuz they're kissing again, stupid," Connor said.

Mary Karen turned in her husband's arms and smiled at the three little boys standing in the doorway.

"You were kissing him," Caleb said. "Is Connor right? Are you happy?"

Mary Karen leaned back against Travis's chest and smiled up at him. "Very happy."

Chapter Thirteen

Mary Karen stared up at her bedroom ceiling. She listened to the sound of running water, trying to decide how she was going to act when Travis joined her in bed.

Even though he said he loved her, she couldn't shake the doubt. After all, Steven had said all the right words, too. Yet in the end he hadn't meant any of them.

If only I could be sure Travis loved me....

"That's a pretty big sigh." Her husband pulled the comforter back and slipped into bed beside her. His hand moved to her belly, touching her tentatively at first, then with more sureness when she didn't push him away. "By Christmas they'll be in a crib down the hall and all we'll have to worry about is getting some sleep."

Even in the dim light she saw the affection in his eyes. Her heart sighed. Travis was clearly trying to make the best of the situation. "I'm going to do everything in my power to make you happy."

She realized she'd spoken louder than she intended when his eyes widened at her outburst. Then he smiled.

"You already make me happy." His fingers, which had been gently caressing her belly, moved upward skimming the edge of her breast. "Every minute…of every hour…of every day."

She fought the flames of desire his touch ignited. "Will you promise to let me know if you ever feel overwhelmed with me or the children?"

Through the silky fabric, his thumb brushed across the sensitive tip of her nipple.

Mary Karen gasped.

"You were saying?"

"If I don't know how you're feeling, I can't make it better," she stammered.

"You'll always know what I'm feeling," he said, moving even closer, his hardness brushing against her leg. "Like now."

Her breath caught, then began again. "I—I'm serious."

"So am I." He scattered kisses up her neck.

Though Mary Karen wanted nothing more than to give in to the desire ravaging her senses, she forced his head up. "Promise me."

His expression turned serious. "On one condition."

"What's that?"

"You promise to do the same. If you don't feel I'm pulling my share, you'll let me know."

Mary Karen hesitated. It should have been

easy to agree, but some of her and Steven's biggest fights had occurred when she'd asked for help. According to him, his job was providing for the family financially, hers was to take care of the house and children.

"There isn't anything you can't say to me." His voice, soft but insistent, broke through her thoughts. "Anything you can't do to me."

She leaned forward and kissed him boldly, slipping her tongue into his mouth.

He reached for her and she went to him, reveling in the feel of his hands on her body, his lips against her skin, knowing no one could love him as much as she did.

"You make me so happy," he murmured.

Mary Karen pulled the gown over her head and tossed it on the floor. Somehow, she'd find a way to make sure he stayed that way.

Mary Karen glanced from the stone fireplace where orange flames danced in the hearth to the large floor-to-ceiling windows offering a panoramic view of Jackson Hole. "I know I've said it before but this is a beautiful home, Lexi. It's stylish and comfortable at the same time."

"Thanks. We like it." Lexi handed Mary Karen a glass of club soda. With effortless ease the beautiful brunette, dressed in a multicolored sweater and black pants, took a seat in one of two leather chairs flanking the fireplace.

Looking at her, Mary Karen would never guess that her friend had given birth less than two months ago. But the baby sleeping upstairs in a fashionable nursery said it was true.

Mary Karen smoothed the front of her red maternity sweater and fought a pang of envy. In the past month, she'd "popped." Her belly— once as flat as Lexi's—now resembled a beach ball. Graceful was no longer a word used to describe the way she moved. Still, the babies were growing and thankfully, so far it had been an uneventful pregnancy.

"David tells me that you and Travis are planning to build nearby." With one finger, July stroked the cheek of her baby son while he nursed. Her sleeping one-year-old lay curled up next to her on the loveseat.

"We met with Joel last week and looked at some plans." Mary Karen remembered Travis's excitement. Okay so she'd been excited, too. A master suite with its own bathroom and huge walk-in closet? What wasn't to love? "Nothing definite has been decided yet."

"Steaks are almost done." Travis sauntered into the room and leaned over to kiss Mary Karen's cheek, his hand sliding down her arm in a possessive gesture. "I bet you're getting hungry."

"I'm doing okay." While Mary Karen tried to moderate her intake, the calories needed to feed two growing babies kept her grazing all day.

"How about these little ones?" Travis rested

a hand on her belly and one of his babies responded with a solid kick.

He grinned. "Definitely a linebacker."

"Or a female kickboxer," Mary Karen said with a laugh.

The invitation to the Labor Day barbecue had indicated lunch would be served at noon. At the last minute the weather had taken a chilly turn and Nick and Lexi had moved the party indoors. The men, not to be dissuaded by a brisk north wind, had decided to brave the elements and grill outside.

"Your wife and babies are in good hands," July assured Travis. "Lexi brought out this fabulous cheese and cracker tray. We've been snacking and sipping."

"On soda," July added with a sigh.

Even though most sources said there was no problem with nursing mothers having an occasional glass of wine, both July and Lexi had deemed alcohol off limits.

"Join us." Mary Karen patted the empty space next to her on the sofa. "Like July said we've got soda. And these yummy snacks."

"Tempting." Travis didn't even glance at the cheese tray. The heat in his eyes told her it wasn't food on his mind.

His continuing passion for her was one of her greatest joys. Of course, as her belly had grown bigger, out of necessity their lovemaking had grown more creative. Last night had been off the charts.

Desire coiled low in her belly. She moistened her lips with the tip of her tongue. "Perhaps later?"

Travis's smile widened. "You can count on it."

"Are you sure you can't stay and keep us company, Travis?" July's green eyes held a decidedly impish gleam. "I'll let you burp the baby."

"Ah, thanks July, but unfortunately I have to pass. I promised the guys I'd bring back some beers. *After* I made sure my wife was okay."

Contentment ran through Mary Karen's veins like warm honey. The past couple months had been the best of her life. She and Travis had begun to build a life together, a wonderful life centered around home and family.

Sometimes it scared her just how easy it was to be his wife. He didn't yell and scream like Steven. The minor issues that had come up had been resolved with conversation. Not only that, the boys had accepted him as their father and his consistent discipline had reduced the chaos in their home.

"Daddy, look here," Logan called up from his position on the floor. "I built me a fort."

Shooting Mary Karen a wink, Travis moved to the boy's side and squatted down, carefully inspecting the lopsided log structure. "Good job, son."

"I'm gonna build a house now. A big house." Logan flung his arms wide. "Just like the one you and Mommy and me and Caleb and Connor are gonna live in. And the itty bitty babies, too."

"I can't wait to see it." Travis tousled the little boy's hair then glanced back at Mary Karen. "The twins?"

"They're downstairs," Lexi answered. "Addie is keeping an eye on them."

"Sounds like you ladies have it under control."

The back door pushed open. "Hey, Trav, did you fall off the mountain? How 'bout those beers?"

"Call me if you need anything, M.K." Travis's gaze met hers and for a second time stood still.

Mary Karen had known this man her whole life, but what they shared now was different, more profound.

After brushing a kiss across her lips, he grabbed three longnecks from the refrigerator then headed outside. She watched until the door closed behind him. When she turned back her friends were staring, knowing smiles lifting their lips.

"He adores you," Lexi said.

"I know," Mary Karen said happily. "I adore him, too."

"What's this I hear about you celebrating Christmas in a couple of weeks?" July raised her infant son to her shoulder and gently rubbed his back.

"It's true." Mary Karen reached forward and grabbed a cracker.

Lexi cocked her head. "Christmas in September?"

"It was actually Travis's idea." Mary Karen nibbled on the cracker. "With the babies due around Christmas, we knew December would be crazy. He didn't want to shortchange the boys so we decided to do the tree and a gift exchange this month and celebrate the real meaning of Christmas in December."

"What a fabulous idea," Lexi said.

July's baby burped his agreement and his mother chuckled.

"We already have the tree up." Mary Karen smiled. They'd all enjoyed the adventure of tromping through the woods, picking out just the right one and cutting it down. "When we get home tonight we're putting up the rest of the decorations. On the twenty-fifth, we'll unwrap the gifts."

"If I knew the sex of the babies, I could pick up a little something for them to go under the tree," July said, a sly look in her eyes.

Lexi stared at Mary Karen with an expectant gaze, ignoring the outside door swinging open and the men entering the kitchen.

Mary Karen wasn't swayed by the pressure. Her parents had used virtually the same tactic. It hadn't worked for them. It wouldn't work now. She lifted her hands. "I really have no idea. Travis and I want to be surprised."

"Surprised?" Nick placed a large platter of

steaks, burgers and hot dogs on the kitchen counter. "About what?"

"The sex of Mary Karen and Travis's babies." July pretended to pout. "She won't tell us."

"Because we don't know," Mary Karen emphasized.

"My extensive medical training tells me they'll either be girls or boys," Travis said. "Or perhaps one of each."

"Gee, thanks, Trav," July drawled. "That narrows it down."

"You know, bro, not knowing is driving my wife crazy," David said.

"An added bonus." Travis shot a teasing look in July's direction.

The banter that followed filled Mary Karen's heart to overflowing. Next to her parents, these people were her support network. Like her, Travis had been part of this tight-knit group of friends for years. Being with him now as part of a couple was an extra blessing.

"Is the food ready yet?" Nine-year-old Addie stuck her head into the kitchen from the door leading downstairs. "The boys are getting wild."

"Bring 'em up." Travis motioned. "We're ready for them."

Utilizing the sofa's armrest, Mary Karen awkwardly pushed herself up to a standing position. "What can I do to help?"

"You can sit back down and rest," Travis said firmly. "I'll get the boys their plates."

"Travis, would you mind first making sure the grill is turned off outside?" Lexi asked.

"You got it."

Mary Karen watched his retreating back and swallowed a sigh. She did love the way her man looked in a pair of jeans.

"I still can't believe that the biggest player in Jackson Hole has turned into such a family man." Lexi shot Mary Karen a teasing smile.

"To think if I hadn't given him a push in the

right direction, it might never have happened."
David chuckled and took a sip of beer.

"Give it up, David," Lexi said. "Those two were meant to be together."

July made some flippant comment about her husband, the consummate matchmaker, and everyone laughed. Everyone except Mary Karen. She couldn't get his comment out of her head.

Push in the right direction? What did it mean?

With a casualness she didn't feel, Mary Karen crossed the room to where her brother stood. "Hey, David, could I speak with you in the other room, please?"

Without giving him a chance to ask any questions—or to turn her down—Mary Karen wrapped her fingers around his arm. She pulled him down the hall, only stopping when she was certain they were out of earshot of the others. "Tell me about this 'push in the right direction.'"

She hoped he would laugh but the shuttered

look in his eyes told her he had something to hide. "It's nothing. I was just joking around."

His mouth said one thing, his eyes something different. Before she could press him for an-swers, the sound of pounding footsteps echoed on the hardwood.

"Mommy, can I have two hot dogs?" Con-nor slipped between Mary Karen and his uncle. "Addie said she gets two."

"Why don't you eat one first, then see how hungry you are after that?" Keeping one eye on her brother, Mary Karen smoothed a blond curl back from her son's face.

David shoved his hands into his pockets and rocked back on his heels. From the look on his face and the longing glance he cast down the hall, her brother would rather be anywhere but with her.

"Tell me," Mary Karen ordered.

"I told you, it was nothing."

"If it's nothing, the story shouldn't take long to tell."

"David," July called out. "I need you."

"Sorry, sis." David turned and headed down the hall, not looking sorry at all.

"Just remember, I know where you live," Mary Karen called after him, only half joking.

Still, she told herself that perhaps it was for the best. Now wasn't the time or the place for such a discussion. She'd get the truth out of her brother. Soon. Very soon.

Chapter Fourteen

The next few weeks passed quickly. Mary Karen thought more about what her brother had said and convinced herself she'd overreacted. She still planned to ask David about it, but she hadn't found the right opportunity to bring it up yet.

The twins had started kindergarten and Logan was in preschool three days a week. She should have had more free time, instead it felt as if all she did was spend her days in the van. She drove the boys to school every morning and picked them up every afternoon. There were times she could have used Travis's help, but his car was a two-seater. The best he could do was to occasionally pick up Logan from preschool.

But Mary Karen didn't mind. Having Travis as her husband had improved her life and lessened her workload by a thousand percent.

She loaded some breakfast plates and glasses into the dishwasher and straightened, her back already starting to ache. She'd been up since six, getting the twins fed and ready for school.

Travis had left the house shortly after she'd gotten up. It was his morning to do surgery. After he finished at the hospital, he had a full afternoon of patient appointments. He'd told her not to expect him before six.

"Looks like it's just you and me today, Logan," she said to her youngest who'd watched while she loaded the dishwasher. "What would you like to do today?"

"Go to the park!" he shouted.

"Shh." Mary Karen brought a finger to her lips. "Remember to use your indoor voice."

"I want to go to the park and play on the monkey bars," the little boy said in a more reasonable tone. "Please, Mommy, can we? Please."

Mary Karen moved to the kitchen window and pushed back the curtains. The fine drizzle that had started to fall during the night was still coming down. Of course, this was Jackson Hole. You only had to wait five minutes and that could change.

"I'm afraid it's raining outside right now, sweetie," she said. "If it clears up this afternoon, we could go then."

Logan thought for a moment and then nodded.

"I could get out your logs," Mary Karen suggested. "You could build me something."

"I want to look at pictures," Logan announced.

It took Mary Karen a second to realize what he meant. Then she remembered the photo albums they'd found in the closet the other day when they'd been cleaning out the spare bedroom, getting it ready for the babies.

That night she and Travis had sat on the sofa with Logan on his lap and the boys on either side. They'd flipped through the albums, looking at photos. All of the ones they'd looked at had been taken after Logan's birth.

Travis had been in many of them. Which wasn't surprising considering that next to her parents and her brother, Travis had helped her the most after Steven had taken off.

"Can we, Mommy?" Logan begged. "Can we look at pictures?"

Mary Karen's back spasmed and she glanced at the sofa in the other room. Although there were dozens of things she wanted to accomplish today, what would it hurt to put her feet up for a few minutes, flip through some photos and spend a little one-on-one time with her child?

"I think that sounds like a swell idea." Mary Karen started toward the living room, her eye on the comfy sofa and ottoman. "Why don't you get an album or two from the bedroom and bring them to me?"

"Okay, Mommy." Logan's face broke into a big smile. "I run fast."

"Walk," she called out as he raced down the hall.

She lowered herself onto the sofa cushions and watched him disappear around the corner. In his striped long-sleeved T-shirt, jeans and sneakers, he looked more like a little boy than her baby.

Soon, Logan would be caught in the middle between one set of older twin siblings and a pair of younger ones. Mary Karen vowed that he would not get overlooked. She would make sure that both she and Travis gave him the attention he deserved.

"I got a big box." Logan shoved a shoebox in her face. "Lots and lots of pictures."

Mary Karen's heart sank. She didn't need to

slip off the lid to know what was inside. These photos were ones taken when Steven was still around.

"Honey." She took the box from her son's hands. "There aren't any pictures of you in here. These are all pictures of your brothers when they were babies."

Logan's blue eyes lit up like the lights on the Christmas tree. He climbed up onto the sofa and settled in next to her. "I wanna see."

Mary Karen stared at the box in her hands. If she was going to take a trip down this particular memory lane, it seemed appropriate that she would do so on a damp, gray-skied day. She lifted the lid off and placed it on the end table.

Logan reached inside and pulled out a handful of loose photos, handing them to her. "I wanna see baby Connor and Caleb."

The first picture she held up was taken in the hospital. She had a baby in each arm and Ste-

ven was sitting beside the bed. Her mother—
or was it her dad?—had taken the family shot.

Mary Karen remembered the photo. Until Steven walked out on her, a copy of this print had sat framed on the fireplace mantel.

Logan giggled. "Your hair looks funny, Mommy."

Mary Karen smiled. Instead of hanging loose to her shoulders like it did now, her hair had been shorter and layered.

She looked young. Innocent. Happy.

Mary Karen remembered the elation she'd felt over giving birth to two healthy babies. She'd been on top of the world, determined to be a fabulous mother and wife.

Logan pointed to Steven. "Who's that?"

"That's your father." She kept her voice matter-of-fact. While Steven would never be her children's daddy, he *was* their father. "He lives in Boston. Remember?"

Logan looked at the man with the dark hair

and tight smile. He tilted his head. "Why is he way over there?"

At first Mary Karen didn't understand what Logan was saying. She glanced down at the familiar photo and studied it, trying to see it through Logan's eyes. Suddenly she understood. It was if she was seeing it for the first time.

Initially she'd assumed Logan was commenting on the fact that Steven wasn't in bed with her and the twins. But now she saw what he meant. Even though Steven's chair was beside the bed, he was leaning *away* from her and his sons rather than toward them.

As she and Logan went through the pictures, the pattern continued. It became apparent that even during the years they'd lived under the same roof, in the same house, he hadn't really been with them. What was worse, she hadn't even noticed.

By the time they got through the box's contents, Logan's eyelids had begun to droop and

Mary Karen's mind was a tangled mess of troubling thoughts and emotions.

Thankfully when she suggested they take a nap, Logan didn't argue. Mary Karen slipped off his sneakers and covered him with a cotton throw. By the time she brushed a kiss across his cheek, he was already asleep.

Though exhaustion wrapped itself around Mary Karen like a weighted vest, she knew she'd never be able to sleep. Not with images of her and Steven running through her mind. And with them the heavy realization that signs of Steven's unhappiness had been there all along.

He'd said he loved her. Not as often as she'd have liked, but enough that she believed him. Of course, he'd also accused her of trapping him into a lifestyle he'd never have chosen, but those hurtful words were said only when he was angry.

She'd always thought it was her unexpected pregnancy with Logan that had pushed him over the edge. Now, she saw that her marriage had been in trouble from the beginning. She'd been so busy trying to be the good mother that she hadn't noticed the signs and addressed the issues before the marriage was irreparably harmed.

Mary Karen swiped a shaky hand across her cheeks, surprised when it came away wet. Pulling a tissue from her pocket, she wiped away the tears then moved to the window and stared out into the grayness.

Was she doing the same thing with this marriage? What had David meant when he'd implied he'd had to give Travis a push?

Mary Karen had made it clear from the beginning that she wouldn't keep him in a marriage he didn't want. And when she'd found out she was pregnant—and his sense of honor and duty had kicked in—she'd asserted she wouldn't settle for anything less than love.

Then he'd told her that he loved her, that he

wanted to be a husband to her and a father to her boys.

A knot formed in the pit of her stomach. Could he have simply told her what she wanted to hear?

No. No. Travis loved her. That's why he was with her now. He hadn't been pushed into this life. He had chosen it. Because he loved her sons and her and their unborn babies.

It was ridiculous to think otherwise. Still, her attempt at a chuckle sounded more like a sob.

She could just ask Travis. But would he be honest? She hated that she had doubts.

Which left David. She would talk to her brother and find out the truth. No matter how painful. Because the one thing she now realized was that sticking her head in the sand didn't work.

"I can't believe you lied to get me over here." David's blue eyes flashed. "Telling me Logan was running a high fever was a low trick."

Mary Karen met his gaze, not intimidated by her brother's annoyance. "I needed to talk with you privately."

David frowned. "What about?"

"What you said at Nick and Lexi's on Labor Day."

"You'll have to be more specific." In a gesture that was as much a part of him as the wave in his hair, her brother jammed his hands into the pockets of his well-worn jeans and rocked back on his heels.

He didn't fool her in the least. The wary look in his eyes told her he knew exactly what comment she meant.

"I made coffee." Mary Karen turned toward the kitchen, hoping he'd follow, relieved when she heard his footsteps behind her on the hardwood.

While she had to know what he'd said to Travis, she had to admit she was scared. What if this wonderful life she'd been living was merely a house of cards ready to tumble down?

Despite her fear she kept her composure and once she reached the kitchen, she poured David a cup of coffee and handed it to him with steady hands.

He wrapped his fingers around the cartoon-character mug and took a cautious sip of the steaming brew. "Aren't you having any?"

"No, because I laced it with truth serum." Despite the seriousness of the situation, Mary Karen smiled at his startled expression. "Just kidding."

"Har, har." David shook his head and took another sip.

"I know this is your day off and that you're eager to get back to July and the kids." Mary Karen kept her tone conversational. "I just want you to tell me what kind of push you gave Travis."

Pulling out a chair, she gestured for David to

take a seat. He sat opposite her, placing his cup on the table.

"You and Trav are happy together," he said. "What else matters?"

For a second Mary Karen was tempted to agree. But knowing she'd spent her first marriage not realizing just how much her husband resented her—and the children—wouldn't let her walk away.

"Remember when July came to Jackson and lied about Adam's paternity? When you found out it nearly tore you two apart. But you finding out was the best thing that could have happened." Mary Karen leaned forward, resting her arms on the table. "Secrets destroy a relationship. I love Travis. I want this marriage to work. But I must know if he's with me because he truly loves me or simply because he feels obligated."

Obligated.

She hated the word.

Tears filled her eyes and spilled down her cheeks.

"Don't cry." David leaned over and awkwardly patted her shoulder. "You're making this out to be a bigger deal than it is."

Mary Karen angrily brushed away the tears and reminded herself that slugging her brother wouldn't get her answers. "David, tell me."

"Let it go, M.K." He shoved back his chair and stood.

"Don't even think about leaving," Mary Karen warned.

"You think you're going to stop me?"

"I'll call July." Mary Karen pulled the cell phone from her pocket and placed it in front of her. "She knows the best thing that ever happened was when that secret finally came out."

David's eyes turned dark. She could almost see him weighing his options.

He sat down and met her gaze. "Let's keep in mind that you were the one who told him you were pregnant but didn't want anything to do with him."

"That isn't how it was." Mary Karen wondered how she'd suddenly ended up being the bad guy. "I just made it clear to Travis that I couldn't bring him into my life—into my boys' lives—if he didn't love me."

"You put the guy in a bad spot, M.K. You're having his baby. He knew you already had your hands full with three kids. What did you expect him to do?"

"I expected him to be honest." Mary Karen rose and leaned forward, planting her hands on the edge of the table. "You, on the other hand, told him to lie if necessary."

David didn't need to respond. The truth was in his eyes.

He reached out to grab her hand, but she jerked it away.

"Don't touch me."

"I didn't tell him to say he loved you."

"Then what did you tell him? I want the exact words."

"I can't remember."

She reached for the phone.

"I told him he'd better do whatever it took to get back in your good graces." David slammed his fist against the table making them both jump. "I was furious with him for putting you in this position."

"Well, I'm furious at *you* for putting me in this position." She'd been so sure Travis was the one. How could she have been wrong twice in a row?

"What are you talking about?"

"I believed Travis when he said he loved me. I let him move in. The boys adore him. How can I ask him to leave now?"

"Why would you do that?" David looked at her as if she'd sprouted wings. "You love him."

"But.he.doesn't.love.me." Mary Karen stopped and took a steadying breath. "I want more for myself. I want what you and July have. What Lexi and Nick have. For the past couple months I thought I had it. But right now I don't know what's true…because my brother *encouraged* my husband to lie to me."

David winced. "I'm sorry, M.K. I never meant to hurt you."

Mary Karen wanted to stay angry with him. Wanted to blame him for allowing her to believe that happily ever after was possible for her.

But she couldn't hold on to the rage. He was her big brother. The one who'd protected her growing up. When Steven had left, he'd been there for her. Yes, he'd made a mistake. But she believed it had been done only with the best of intentions.

"Thanks for finally being honest with me." Avoiding his searching gaze, she headed down the hall. When she reached the front door, she turned. "Tell July hello."

"You and Travis have a good thing going."

His voice was low and filled with anguish. "I hope I didn't screw it up."

"You didn't screw anything up, David." She kissed his cheek and pushed him out the front door. "Travis did."

Chapter Fifteen

Mary Karen buckled Logan into his car seat then slipped behind the wheel of the aging mini-van. After she picked up the twins from school, they'd stop at the store. Shopping with three little kids wasn't her idea of fun, but it couldn't be helped. The cupboards were almost bare. By the time she got home it would be time to start dinner.

Then Travis would be home.

Normally she couldn't wait for him to walk

through the door. But right now she wasn't sure what she would say, how she was going to act.

The child in her wanted to slam the door in his face and tell him she never wanted to see him again. The adult in her knew that wouldn't solve anything.

Mary Karen slipped the key into the ignition and as she bent over, she caught a glimpse of her twenty-six-year-old face in the rearview mirror.

Passably pretty.

A dutiful daughter.

A loyal friend.

A mother who tried her best.

All she wanted was a husband she loved and who loved her back.

She could see now that she'd never have had that kind of life with Steven. His violent outbursts. The verbal abuse.

Best friends?

Soul mates?

Mary Karen snorted. She hadn't known how truly unhappy she'd been until Steven was out of her life.

Travis was different. He was the whole package; a decent, honorable man who was sweet and caring and passionate. *He* was her soul mate. Her best friend.

Had he given up the life he wanted for her? She wouldn't know until he got home and they had a chance to talk.

With a resigned sigh, she turned the key.

Then turned it again.

Flipped the key back and tried one more time.

Dead silence.

She glanced at her watch and bit back an expletive. In fifteen minutes her two five-year-olds would be out in front of the school waiting for her to pick them up.

Her first impulse was to call Travis. She immediately dismissed that option. His Roadster wasn't big enough to handle both boys.

She grabbed her cell phone from her bag and hit Speed Dial, praying her mom would answer. Their van not only had the room, it had child seats for each of the boys.

Within minutes she had the pickup arranged. There was barely any food in the house for dinner but that couldn't be helped. Her children's safety and a dead battery took priority.

Sometimes a woman just had to play the cards she'd been dealt.

"Tofu pizza?" Travis stared down at the slice on his plate and tried not to cringe.

Mary Karen took a sip of milk. "It's either that or nothing."

There was an edge to her voice that had been there since he got home. Though she'd tried to conceal her red, swollen eyes with makeup, he'd noticed them immediately. He'd asked about her day but all he'd gotten was a clipped "Fine."

"I thought you were going to the store today."

He forked off a bite but couldn't bring himself to lift the piece to his mouth. Still, since she'd gone to the trouble to make it, he'd have to find a way to gag it down.

He wondered if this was payback for the night he'd given Kate a ride to his welcome back party. If so, Mary Karen couldn't have picked a worse day. He'd been so busy, he'd skipped lunch. Still, he'd promised not to complain so he clamped his mouth shut and ignored the piece of slime on his plate.

"I planned on grocery shopping this afternoon." She shot a steely-eyed look at the twins who were mashing down the topping on their slices of pizza. "I didn't make it to the store."

"The van wouldn't start." Logan picked up his glass of milk, dragging his sleeve across the top of his pizza in the process. "Mommy called Grandma, then she cried and cried."

The twins looked up and exchanged glances. Travis pulled his brows together. This was the first he'd heard of car trouble. He put down his fork. "Honey, what happened?"

"When I tried to start the car, the battery was dead," she said as if it had been of no consequence, certainly not something that had made her "cry and cry." "I called my mother and she picked up the twins for me. Then I called the Battery Store."

"Why didn't you call me?" he asked. "I could—"

"What could you have done?" Mary Karen paused, then offered a slight smile as if to offset the abruptness of her response. "Finding someone to pick up the boys was my first concern. Once I had that covered, all that was left was having a new battery brought out and installed. No worries. I'm more than capable of handling these kinds of minor catastrophes. After all, I've been on my own since Steven left."

"You're not on your own anymore." He leaned over and took her hand. "I'm sorry you had to deal with it alone. I wish I would have been here to help."

She slipped her hand from his and he caught a glimpse of something in her eyes that he didn't understand. Pain? Hurt? Anger? All three emotions?

"Maybe you should kiss Mommy and make it all better," Connor suggested.

Travis wasn't fooled. The boy wasn't so much interested in seeing his mother kissed as he was in diverting attention from the pizza he was stuffing in his napkin.

Logan's brows pulled together in worry. "I don't want Mommy to cry again."

"I don't, either." Travis stood and rounded the table, taking Mary Karen's hand again and pulling her to her feet.

She rose with obvious reluctance.

Her hesitation surprised him. Something was definitely troubling her.

He cupped her face with one hand then gently covered her mouth with his. She allowed it for a second then stepped away.

"All better," she said, smiling at her sons. A smile that didn't quite reach her eyes.

A chill traveled up his spine. Travis wasn't sure if Mary Karen's somber mood was simply pregnancy hormones or something else. But because the boys were watching, he pretended he hadn't noticed anything amiss. Over dinner he smiled and joked and even managed to down a piece of pizza.

With three sets of ears hanging on their every word, there was no opportunity to talk privately.

Once the boys were asleep and Mary Karen was in the bedroom changing, Travis set into motion his plan to bolster her spirits. He started by opening a bottle of sparkling grape juice and splashing some into two wineglasses. The lights on the Christmas tree added a festive glow to the living room. He lit a couple of candles. Soon the smell of cinnamon and spices filled the air. After turning on Kenny G's Christmas album, Travis stepped back and studied the room.

Perfect. If this didn't cheer his wife up, he was out of ideas.

Mary Karen entered the room then paused, her mouth forming a perfect O. Her hair gleamed like spun gold in the muted light. Dressed in a silky blue gown and robe with bits of lace at the neck and cuffs, she looked as lovely as the angel topping the tree.

Pleased with her reaction, Travis smiled and handed her a glass. "I thought it'd be nice to celebrate."

Mary Karen stared at the drink in her hand then raised her gaze. "Celebrate what?"

"It's exactly three months until our babies are due." He smiled. "I thought you'd be counting down the days."

She ignored his teasing grin and took a seat

in the chair, rather than her normal spot next to him on the sofa.

"Is that what you're doing, Travis?" she asked quietly. "Counting down the days?"

Travis wasn't sure what she meant, so he didn't answer her question directly. He'd been around women enough to know what they said often had no connection to what was really troubling them.

"If you'd have called, I'd have figured out a way to pick up the twins." Travis dropped down on the sofa cushion, hating the thought of how stressed she'd been. It wasn't good for her or the babies to be so upset. "You shouldn't have had to—"

"This has nothing to do with the boys." She picked at the lace on her sleeve. "I talked with David this morning."

An odd remark. Her brother and sister-in-law couldn't be an issue. She had a great relationship with both of them. Unless there was something going on with Adam or Alex… "Is everything okay with the kids?"

"As far as I know they're fine."

Travis understood that there was something his wife wanted to say. Some reason her family had stopped over. What he didn't understand was why she didn't just tell him. Why he had to pry it out of her. He forced a smile and tried again. "Any special reason they stopped over?"

"Not July. Just my brother. And he came because I asked," Mary Karen said. "We talked about you."

Suddenly all this cat-and-mouse action made sense. Mary Karen had been stressing for weeks over what gift to get him. Ever since they'd decided to celebrate Christmas in September, she'd been asking in some subtle and not-so-subtle ways what he wanted. Since he hadn't given her any suggestions, it appeared she'd decided to try to get some ideas from her brother.

"Honestly, M.K., don't worry about getting me a gift. Just having you and the boys—"

"I didn't ask him over to find out what you'd like for a gift." She shifted her gaze to the tree with the twinkling lights for several seconds before refocusing on him. "David made a comment a couple weeks ago at Lexi and Nick's Labor Day barbecue. About you."

Travis cocked his head. Just when he thought he had it all figured out, the conversation veered in a totally different direction. "What did he say?"

Mary Karen's eyes met his. "Something to the effect that he didn't think we'd be together if he hadn't pushed you in the right direction."

Relaxing against the back of the sofa, Travis shook his head. "That's your brother. Trying to take credit for us being together. He's been trying to match us up for years." He laughed, recalling David's awkward and not-so-subtle attempts to bring him and Mary Karen together.

"Remember that time in college when you had that sorority dance and he—"

"That's not it at all." Mary Karen expelled a harsh breath.

"Then what?" Travis's smile faded at the serious look blanketing her face.

She leaned forward, as far as her belly would allow, pinning him with her gaze. "When he found out I was pregnant, did he—or did he not—tell you to do whatever it took to convince me to let you be a part of my life?"

Travis furrowed his brow. He remembered David's anger that day—and the locker latch digging into his back—but his friend's exact words were a little hazy. "He may have said something to that effect, yes. I know he was quite upset."

The last bit of hope in her eyes disappeared. "That's why you told me you loved me."

While he may have set out to deliberately win Mary Karen over, Travis knew what David had said hadn't had any real impact on his actions. "I told you I loved you because it's true."

"Really?"

He ignored the skepticism in her tone.

"I believe that I've always loved you." The moment he said the words a sense of peace settled over him. "You've been one of my closest friends for as far back as I can remember."

The smile that had begun to lift her lips disappeared. "I don't want you to love me as a friend."

Now he was thoroughly confused. "What are you talking about?"

Her blue eyes flashed. "Actions, Trav, speak louder than words."

"Haven't I showed you how much I love you? When we're in bed together—"

"You were all about a divorce until you found out I was pregnant." Mary Karen jerked to her feet and crossed the room.

Travis rose and quickly moved to her side,

standing as close as he dared. He had a bad feeling he was making matters worse. If only he understood why. "Mary Karen, honey, where is all this coming from?"

"The reason—the *only* reason—you told me you loved me was because you felt an obligation, a duty, to me and the babies." Her voice started out shaky but grew stronger with each word. "You made me believe— Well, anyway, I know better now. There's no need for you to pretend I'm anything more than just an obligation."

He took a chance and slipped his arms around her, pulling her close. "I love you," he said with a fierceness that surprised him as much as it did her. "The fact that you were first my friend doesn't diminish the feelings I now have for you."

Curling a finger beneath her chin he urged it upward until her gaze met his. "What do I have to do to convince you I'm sincere?"

Mary Karen stared into his eyes for a long moment before answering. "Tell me you'd have wanted to stay married and be a father to my boys even if I hadn't been pregnant."

He hesitated, wanting to be honest. "I can't say that for sure, but I can tell you that I've been extremely happy being a family man these past four months."

She sighed. "I put you in the position where you had to marry me."

"That's simply not true, M.K.," he said, keeping his tone light. "Correct me if I'm wrong but I don't recall anyone putting a gun to our heads in that wedding chapel."

"But we were going to get a divorce—"

"We didn't."

"Because of the babies."

"Because," he stressed, "we realized we loved each other."

"I want to believe you, Trav. But I—I can't."

Her eyes were filled with such despair that

he couldn't be angry. On the stereo, Kenny G's sax belted out, "Have Yourself a Merry Little Christmas."

"Helluva thing," Travis muttered.

"What is?"

"To be in love with your wife and not have her believe you."

Chapter Sixteen

Travis stood at the door to her bedroom—*their* bedroom, darn it—with a bath towel wrapped around his waist and prayed Mary Karen would be asleep when he walked into the room. He'd stayed in the shower until his skin had started to take on the unappealing characteristics of a prune, wanting to give her enough time to fall asleep.

Not that he didn't want to talk things out— he did—it was just that they were both tired.

All those years of raising teenagers had taught Travis a few things about conflict resolution.

Regardless of what some relationship books said about not going to bed with unresolved issues, he'd learned that when you reach an impasse, it's often best to defer further discussion until the morning. A good night's sleep often made seemingly insurmountable problems, workable. Tomorrow, in the bright light of a new day, Mary Karen would realize she'd been foolish to doubt his love.

I hope.

Holding his breath, he slipped inside the room and pulled the door closed with as much stealth as he could muster. Then he glanced at the bed.

It was empty.

For a second a frisson of panic shot up his spine and he feared Mary Karen was gone. Until he realized that was ridiculous. This was her house. And, while she might leave him,

she'd never leave the three little boys sleeping
down the hall.

At the same instant the reassuring thought
crossed his mind, he saw her. She sat in a chair
by the window, watching him with an unreadable expression, her hands folded in her lap.

"I thought you'd be asleep."

"You mean you *hoped* I'd be asleep," she said.

"If you're implying I don't want to resolve
this, this misunderstanding, you're mistaken,"
he said stiffly.

"I don't want to argue."

"That's not what I want, either." Keeping his
gaze focused on Mary Karen, he crossed the
room and sat on the bed. "Our relationship, our
marriage, is important to me. I hope you know
that you can always count on me."

Travis kept his voice even in an attempt to
diffuse the tension filling the room.

"David was right." Her gaze dropped to her

hands, her voice barely audible. "I brought this on myself."

"What do you mean?" he kept his voice equally soft and low.

She lifted her gaze, her beautiful blue eyes filled with regret. "He said I'd put you in a no-win situation by saying you had to love me or I wouldn't stay married to you. He said I gave you no choice but to lie."

David was going to have some explaining to do, the next time Travis saw him. But he didn't have time to dwell on his brother-in-law's comments now. "I didn't lie to you. I—"

Mary Karen raised a hand. "I owe you an apology. I put you in a bad position with my demand. It was silly and certainly not fair. I want to assure you that regardless of what happens between you and me, you can have as much access to your babies as you want. We can even partner in their upbringing, if that's what you want."

Partner in their upbringing?

Travis couldn't believe what he was hearing. His stomach clenched. Was she really thinking about them not being together? Planning a…divorce? He cleared his throat and met her gaze. "You know what I want. I want us to be together…the boys…the babies…you and me. The way it has been. That's the way I like it. It's the way it should be for us."

Though he tried to keep it under control, his voice shook with emotion. At the moment, he didn't care. His entire life was on the chopping block. His future happiness was at stake.

"I know you worry about me." She played with the ribbons on her gown and offered him a wan smile. "You want to protect me. But I'll be okay. I'm a strong person. And I'm blessed with a strong family support system."

"What about me?" He leaned forward. "I'm your family. I'm here for you."

"I know you are." Unexpectedly she lifted her

hand and caressed his cheek with the back of her fingers.

His hopes rose. Travis reached for her hand but she pulled it back out of reach.

"I want you to take some time to think about what it is you really want." She squared her shoulders and a look of resolve crossed her face. "I don't want you to be a little bit or mostly in this relationship. I want more than that. I deserve more than that."

There was a finality to her tone that he hadn't heard before. "Are you telling me to leave?"

"No, but I'm not asking you to stay, either."

Travis let out the breath he'd been holding. It wasn't quite the answer he'd hoped for but at least she wasn't telling him to pack his bags.

"If you choose to live here while making your decision, we won't be intimate." She chewed on her lower lip for a second, then continued, her gaze steady, "And, if we do split up, we won't be going back to the whole friends-with-benefits thing. That's over. Done. Finished. Kaput. I told myself it was just sex, and that neither of us would get hurt. But I was wrong. It was more, at least for me. I'm through lying to myself."

By now Travis's head was spinning. He wondered when he was going to wake up from this nightmare. "I love you, M.K."

Her eyes searched his. "I think maybe you do. But how much? Enough that you're right where you want to be? That's the question you need to answer."

"I can answer that now," he said, taking a chance and pulling her close, relief flooding him when she didn't immediately pull away. "I—"

Her fingers closed over his lips and she shook her head. "No. Take the time. Search your heart. Be honest with yourself and then with me. Remember, no matter what you decide, you won't lose contact with your babies or with me. I'll always be your friend."

* * *

He would continue on as if nothing had changed.

It wasn't much of a plan but after tossing and turning most of the night, it was the only plan Travis could come up with by the time the clock chimed six.

Taking great care not to wake Mary Karen, he dressed quickly and slipped out of the bedroom. She'd barely slept last night, too, but had finally fallen into an exhausted slumber about three o'clock.

The past couple of hours had told Travis that, for him, sleep wasn't happening. Try as he might to shut it off, his mind kept searching for a solution, trying to figure out what he could *do* to show her that he was right where he wanted to be. But there seemed to be no answer…other than to stay the course.

Why couldn't she just enjoy the life they were building together and believe that he was no longer that fool who'd eschewed marriage and fatherhood?

He reached the living room and sat down to pull on his boots, realizing if he were her he'd also have difficulty believing the one-eighty he'd done was sincere. Especially in light of her brother's comments.

The truth was, being a husband and a father had been so incredibly easy that he wondered why he'd resisted it for so long. Being with M.K. and the boys had filled a void in his life that he hadn't even known was there.

Sure he'd enjoyed his years of freedom but when he'd met up with Mary Karen in Vegas, a part of him had realized she was what he wanted, what he'd always wanted and he had to have her. As his wife. As the mother of his children.

Now, he just had to figure out a way to convince her of his sincerity. What had she said? Actions speak louder than words? It was too bad she'd nixed the lovemaking because he could think of lots of ways in bed that he could show her his love.

Still, he'd continue to look for another way. Because he loved this woman and her three little boys with his whole heart. Failure wasn't an option.

After a restless night, Mary Karen rose the next morning, determined to spend the day cleaning. Scrubbing floors, vacuuming and picking up toys on what looked to be a beautiful Saturday didn't make much sense but she needed to keep busy. The activities would hopefully stop her from thinking, from feeling, from imagining what her life would be like without Travis.

Not that he'd given any indication at breakfast that he was thinking of leaving. He made scrambled eggs and bacon for her and the boys, like he did every morning he didn't have to rush off to the hospital. Teased her and the boys just like any other morning. But she saw the shadows in his eyes and knew he hadn't slept much, either.

It was hard to summon up much sympathy. Feeling his warm body beside her had been absolute torture. He could have at least had the consideration to put on a pair of pajamas. Several times during the long, lonely hours she'd had to stop herself from reaching for him. She longed to cast away her fears and lose herself in his arms. But each time she'd somehow managed to keep her hands to herself, knowing the issue standing between them wasn't something that sex—no matter how fabulous—could solve. And interjecting it into the equation while he was searching his soul would only complicate matters.

Heaving a sigh, she grabbed a mop from the utility closet. She hoped Travis had somewhere to go today. If he saw her cleaning he'd be shocked…and then angry. He'd made it clear last month that he was taking over all the household chores. Her only job was to rest, relax and let the babies grow.

Mary Karen hadn't argued. Not then. In fact, she'd been relieved and hard-pressed not to cheer. But now that her short-lived happiness was crumbling down around her, she had to do something to keep herself occupied. Something to still the pain bubbling up inside her. Even if that meant cleaning. Ugh. She grimaced and reached for the cleaning solution. Her cell phone rang just as she curved her fingers around a bottle of floor cleaner. She smiled, recognizing July's ring, grateful for the brief reprieve.

"Hey, you," she answered then unconsciously stiffened when Travis entered the room. "What's up?"

As she'd anticipated Travis's smile immediately faded when he caught sight of the bucket, rubber gloves and floor cleaner. Disapproval blanketed his face and he gently confiscated the cleaning solution from her hands.

"No," he mouthed, shaking his head.

Her heart pounded so hard at his nearness, she missed July's question.

"I'm sorry, July, what did you say?" she asked, ignoring Travis and concentrating on the phone in her hand. "I guess I—I could go," she stammered. "Let me ask Trav."

She turned to the man who was—for now—still her husband. In his jeans and striped pullover shirt the young doctor looked way too handsome and put together for nine o'clock in the morning. His arms were crossed as he leaned against the counter, watching her with an inscrutable expression.

She brushed a strand of tangled hair back from her face, knowing she looked a mess and wishing she'd at least put on some makeup. "July has asked me to go with her to the arts festival downtown."

"Sounds like fun," he said, his eyes never leaving her face. "Do you want to go?"

Actually, earlier in the week she'd planned on asking him to go with her, but baby brain had kicked in and she'd forgotten all about it.

The QuickDraw Art Sale and Auction brought together local and regional artists. They set up in the town square and spectators could watch them paint and sculpt. Afterward, the artwork was auctioned off.

It had been years since Mary Karen had attended the event. She'd thought about going last year but the image of Connor knocking over some sculpture, or Caleb getting into someone's paints had dissuaded her.

"I'd like to go," she said slowly. "But July wants it to be a girls' day out. That means I'll need someone to watch the boys."

"I can watch them," Travis said. "I'm not on call today."

"I don't know." Mary Karen hesitated. "They're not your responsibility—"

"What do you mean? Of course they're my responsibility." Then, as if realizing his tone had been a bit harsh, he offered a conciliatory smile. "It'll be good for you to get out of the house and spend time with a friend."

"Hey, you two, listen to me. I don't want to cause trouble—" July's voice sounded from the phone still cupped in Mary Karen's palm.

"Hold on, July," Mary Karen said, not taking her eyes off Travis. "Are you sure? You really want to spend the day babysitting?"

"I don't want no stinkin' babysitter," Connor shouted from the doorway. "Especially not mean Erin."

"Super-mean Erin," Caleb echoed, following his twin into the room.

"Connor. Watch your language. That goes for you, too, Cal," Travis said, a definite warning in his voice. "Erin is a very nice girl."

"I got your truck. I got your truck." Logan peered around the corner, holding out the shiny red vehicle, taunting his brothers with the toy.

Connor's eyes widened. He and Caleb exchanged a horrified glance.

Logan's dimples flashed.

"That's mine," Connor yelled, taking off running with his twin on his heels.

Logan laughed and disappeared into the hall as his brothers thundered from the room.

"Walk," Travis called after the boys. "And try not to kill each other."

Mary Karen hid a smile. Sometimes it was easy for her to take for granted just how good Travis was with children. Firm, always fair, but with a definite sense of humor. "You sure you want to watch the little monsters?"

"They'll mellow out," he said with a confident smile. "I've wanted to take them fishing for a long time. I think today would be a good day to go."

"Thank you, Travis." Mary Karen smiled at him then lifted the phone to her ear. "July, I'm sorry to keep you waiting but it's good news. It's a go."

They spoke for a few minutes longer, finalizing the arrangements. Mary Karen was about to hang up when Travis held out his hand.

She cast him a questioning glance.

"I need to speak with David."

Her heart stopped beating for several seconds. Mary Karen thought of how angry he'd been at her brother last night. Her fingers tightened around the phone. "I'm not sure now is a good time."

The words had barely left her lips when Travis lifted the phone from her fingers.

"Hi, July. I need you to do me a favor," he said smoothly. "Ask your husband if he'd like to go fishing with me and the boys."

Within minutes, all plans were in place. Since

July was going to stop over in thirty minutes, Mary Karen had to scramble to get ready.

When she returned to the dining room, Travis had the room picked up and the boys dressed and ready to go. Mary Karen could tell the twins were excited by the way they kept punching each other.

"You look very nice," he said, gazing appreciatively at her new cinnamon-colored maternity sweater and pants.

"I even put on some makeup." She batted her lashes at him, before she remembered she shouldn't flirt.

He apparently didn't have any such compunction. His smile widened and his eyes began to twinkle.

"Love the tail," he said, giving the hair she'd pulled back and curled, a gentle tug.

A rush of pleasure washed over Mary Karen and she couldn't help from smiling back.

"M.K.," he began. "I hope you know—"

"What's David doing with the children?" Mary Karen hated to interrupt but she refused to get into a heavy discussion only minutes before July showed up.

"He called back a few minutes ago," Travis said. "Your parents are coming over to his home to babysit. I told David I'd stop by and pick him up."

Although everything was in place, now that the time was here, guilt sluiced through Mary Karen. Here she'd told him last night to think if he really wanted to be a husband and a father and now she was foisting three rowdy boys on him on his day off. Talk about torpedoing yourself. "Are you positive you don't mind?"

"Are you talking about me watching our boys?" Travis tossed a duffle bag onto the table. "Or me taking the van?"

"Both." Since David's SUV wasn't big enough to handle two men, three kids and fishing tackle, Travis had no choice but to take the van. Since she and July would walk downtown, they didn't need a vehicle.

"I know you love Ethel, but I promise I'll take good care of her." He sounded surprisingly serious. Then he grinned. "Oh, and I'll take good care of the kids, too."

Travis had proven to be an able father in the past few months so Mary Karen wasn't worried about that at all. She just hated that he was forced to take Ethel. "Thank you for not complaining about the van."

His brows pulled together in puzzlement. "Why would I complain?"

A knock sounded on the door, sparing her the need to respond. "I bet that's July."

Travis pushed aside the lace curtain with one hand and peered out. "Yep, she's here."

Mary Karen started toward the door, but before she'd taken two steps, Travis grabbed her hand and pulled her back, kissing her soundly.

Hadn't she told him no kissing? No, wait,

she'd told him no sex. Her fingers rose to her still tingling lips. "What was that for?"

"I love you and don't you forget it."

Chapter Seventeen

July glanced away from the abstract sculpture. "He said that?"

Resisting the urge to touch her lips like a love-struck adolescent, Mary Karen nodded.

"Then…I'd believe him," her sister-in-law said with a decisive nod.

"You would?"

July twisted a strand of auburn hair around her finger. "When I was seeing Dr. Allman last year—trying to get up the courage to tell David the truth—he said that when David told me he loved me, I should believe him. It's called taking people at face value."

"Steven told me he loved me, but he didn't," Mary Karen said pointedly. She didn't want to be a Debbie Downer, but life wasn't as simple as Dr. Allman's advice implied.

Before July could respond, the crowd surged forward, the momentum pushing Mary Karen off balance. Her sister-in-law grabbed her arm, stopping her fall.

"How about we get a coffee or something?" July dodged a woman's suitcase-size purse and a feisty white furball on a pink leash. "You'd think after living in downtown Chicago all those years I'd be used to crowds, but I'm not. Unless you prefer to stay and watch—"

"I'm getting a bit claustrophobic, too." Mary Karen placed a hand to her back. "And I'm definitely ready to get off my feet."

Mary Karen hadn't even finished speaking when July crooked her arm through hers and they began weaving their way through the throng of people. Though it wasn't far, by the time they reached the coffee shop, Mary Karen's breath came in short puffs. She bit back an exclamation of dismay when she saw that, like the streets, the shop was packed with people.

"Those girls are getting up." July pointed. "You snag the table by the window, I'll order. What can I get you?"

"Green tea," Mary Karen called over her shoulder.

Several minutes later July joined her. She handed Mary Karen her drink then took a seat on the other side of the small round table.

Mary Karen took a sip of the steaming tea, surprised when her sister-in-law simply stared at her cappuccino making no move to drink it.

"What's the matter?"

July looked up, her eyes serious. "There's no delicate way to say this."

"Say what?"

"Don't let your ex ruin your life."

Mary Karen tilted her head. "I'm not following."

"From what you've told me, Steven made the three years you were married pretty miserable."

Mary Karen nodded, still not sure where this was headed.

"From where I'm sitting, he's still doing it."

"No," Mary Karen protested. "I haven't even seen him in—"

"Time doesn't matter. The lies he told you are now making you doubt Travis. Your husband says he loves you, but you don't believe him… because of your experiences with Steven," July said. "Never give a rat that power."

"But what if Travis gets tired of being with me? Or being a dad? What if he—"

"What if you could be blissfully happy but instead you choose to spend your time worrying about what *might* happen?"

July made it sound simple. But that's because

she and David were so happy, so in love, that her sister-in-law thought it was possible for everyone.

"Can we change the subject, please?" Mary Karen may have phrased it as a question but this discussion was over. While she didn't doubt her friend's sincerity, July didn't understand, couldn't understand. After all, July had married a man who *wanted* to be with her.

Her sister-in-law opened her mouth, then paused.

Mary Karen braced herself, knowing that just because she'd asked July to drop it, didn't mean she would.

"Have you decided what you're getting Travis for your Christmas celebration?"

The celebration. She'd nearly forgotten about it.

Mary Karen expelled the breath she didn't realize she'd been holding. "Rubber car mats. For his BMW."

July tilted her head and wrinkled her nose.

"To protect the carpeting," Mary Karen explained. "You know how wet and sloppy it gets around here."

"But car mats?" July didn't bother hiding her dismay. "Isn't that sort of like him getting you a blender?"

"Maybe," Mary Karen reluctantly agreed. "But at the time I chose the mats specifically so he could see I support him having a sports car."

Now she wondered if it even mattered.

"When you explain it that way it does make sense." July swiped the whipped cream off the top of her drink with her finger, then brought it to her lips for a brief taste. "By the way, I emailed you the pictures I took at Lexi's Labor Day bash. There were some good ones of you and Travis."

July had been a photojournalist when she and David had first met. Her camera came with her to every family event and her keen eye made even the simplest digital photo spectacular. "I can't wait to see them. Thank you."

They talked for a while about friends Rachel and Derek Rossi in California who were hoping to return to Jackson Hole, then moved on to John and Kayla Simpson's little girl who was facing another heart surgery.

Even though Mary Karen had known July less than two years, it felt as if they'd been friends forever. She couldn't imagine her brother picking anyone who'd have fit better into the family.

"Yikes." July held up her phone showing Mary Karen the time. "I promised your parents I'd be home ten minutes ago."

"Then I guess we better go." Mary Karen pushed back her chair and stood, reluctant to have the outing end. She'd have to remember to thank Travis again. She hadn't realized how much she missed having girl time. "This was fun. We'll have to do this again."

"Again and often." July looped an arm through hers. "The men can watch the kids."

Mary Karen saw no need to mention that her man might not be around all that much longer. Not only because it might ruin what was left of their outing, but if she said the words, she might start crying.

"You think they'll be angry at me for being late?" July asked with a worried little frown when they reached the door.

"If I know my mom and dad they won't want to give those babies back." Mary Karen chuckled. "I bet Dad is showing Adam his HO train set while Alex is probably getting lots of cuddle time with Mom."

"Something tells me you're right." July grinned. "I wonder if those two ever thought they'd have five grandsons."

"They're so good with them, it's hard to imagine them without all those little boys to spoil." Mary Karen patted her protruding belly as they stepped onto the sidewalk. "Something tells me I'm going to be adding even more testosterone to the mix."

"You're having boys?" July stopped suddenly and whirled. "And you didn't tell me?"

"I don't know that *for sure*," Mary Karen clarified. "It's just that my intuition tells me they're boys."

July's green eyes turned curious. "Is that what you and Travis are hoping for?"

You and Travis. July put their names together as if they were a perfect fit. If only that were true.…

"Mary Karen?" July prompted.

"It really doesn't matter as long as they're healthy." She thought of that awful scare early in her pregnancy and remembered how glad she'd been to have Travis there. "Trav doesn't care either way. I told him I'd like to have at least one girl but I'd be happy with more boys, too."

They sidestepped around a woman waiting with a double stroller outside the ice cream shop next door.

"I can't believe you're going to be a mother of five," July mused.

"Sometimes I find it hard to believe." She watched a man—obviously the woman's husband—hurrying to her with a cone in each hand. "Having Travis at my side these past few months has made parenting a zillion times easier."

"That much better, huh?"

"I can't imagine life without him," Mary Karen said simply as an ache filled her heart at the thought of losing him. "I only hope he feels the same way."

After arguing good-naturedly about the best fishing spot in Yellowstone, David and Travis finally agreed on Lewis River.

Before they brought out the gear they took

the boys for a hike, hoping to dissipate some of their boundless energy. Once the three stopped running and began walking, it seemed time to get the poles out of the van and the hooks in the water.

Helping the twins and Logan get situated on the bank brought back memories of the times Travis had taken his siblings fishing. In medical school—when life had been hectic and filled with stress—sitting at the edge of a lake in the quiet sunshine had been one of the few ways he'd found to totally relax.

"This winter we'll have to take the twins with us when we go snowmobiling." Travis had no doubt zooming through the mountains would be something the boys would enjoy. "They're old enough."

Every winter he and a bunch of his buddies brought their snowmobiles to the park. There were hundreds of miles of trails to bump and bounce over. He smiled, thinking of the fun he was going to have exploring Yellowstone with the twins.

"Are you serious?" David said in a low tone as if worried the boys might overhear.

"Don't you think they'd enjoy it?"

"Ah, they'd have a blast. It's just more work when you have a kid riding with you. A *lot* more work."

Travis glanced at Connor and Caleb who were busy throwing stones in the river and scaring the fish away. "I don't mind."

Of course, that was assuming he was still around. Mary Karen could throw him out any day now. Travis shoved the thought aside. He *would* be around. For Mary Karen and for the boys.

"Just remember you and Mary Karen are going to be busy with two new babies this winter," David said pointedly.

"I can't wait." Even though Travis spoke to

David, he kept his eyes on the three boys. "It'll be a lot of work but it will be worth it."

"You know, Trav, for a guy who didn't want kids, you seem to have jumped into fatherhood with both feet."

"Being with M.K. and the boys feels…right," Travis said.

"You really *are* happy with my sister."

Travis nodded then grimaced. "Too bad she doesn't believe I am."

David cast his line into the water with well-practiced ease. "What do you mean?"

"It's a combination of things." Travis shrugged, deliberately being vague. When they'd been walking the trails with the boys earlier, David had brought up his comment to Mary Karen. Travis saw that his friend felt badly and had accepted his apology without mentioning the ultimatum Mary Karen had given him. "It's like M.K. is trying too hard, determined not to put any demands on me."

Or at least she had been trying…until last night when she'd laid it on the line.

David raised a brow.

"I'll give you an example. Mary Karen ran into a problem the other day with the van not starting. She didn't call me because I couldn't have picked up the boys anyway. Yet she didn't say a word about how impractical a two-seater is when you already have three kids. She was being, well, too nice."

His friend's expression turned serious. "I think she feels guilty over 'trapping' you and is trying to do everything she can to keep you happy."

"She didn't trap me."

"I know that. You know that. But my sister is a worrier."

"You've got that right," Travis said.

"The only way it's going to stop is when she finally truly believes you want to be with her and the boys."

Travis stared out over the water. He heard the high, excited voices of the children and prayed for a revelation. There had to be something he could do, something he could say to convince M.K. he was right where he wanted to be.

The answer came unexpectedly when they were loading up the van, getting ready to leave.

David took a step back and gazed fondly at the van. "Say what you want about Ethel, our SUV wouldn't be able to handle these kids and the cargo."

"She's a good old girl." Travis patted the side of the battle-scarred vehicle. "You need a van like this for a large family."

"I'm surprised you even want to be seen in this bloated beast," David teased. "You've certainly made no secret of your dislike for all things minivan."

"You're right about that." Travis had no doubt that's why M.K. had been so shocked when he'd asked to use it. But his previous attitude had been before he had a family and could appreciate all the advantages.

David chuckled. "I know you'll hate this comparison but in that way you and Steven are alike. He hated Ethel with a passion. The van symbolized everything he didn't like about the life he was living."

"Daddy?"

Travis looked down at the circle of boys clustered around him. Their shirts were dirty, their hair held grass and twigs. He wasn't sure who'd spoken and it didn't matter. They were all his sons.

"We want to come again," Connor said, looking uncharacteristically solemn.

"Con promises not to go into the water again." Caleb nudged his brother and his twin nodded.

""n I won't cry," Logan added.

"Those hooks are sharp." Travis put a reassuring hand on the boy's shoulder, seeing no need to mention that he'd told Logan not to pick it up.

"Will you bring us again?" Caleb pressed.

"Of course." Travis's heart swelled with emotion. "And next year we'll bring the babies so they can watch their big brothers fish."

The boys talked about everything they were going to show their baby brothers while David and Travis got them buckled in. He didn't bother to remind them they might get one or two girls. If that happened, he and Mary Karen would deal with their sons' disappointment. Together.

Travis slid the van door shut and stood for a second, the sun shining through the fir trees warming his face. A feeling of contentment stole over him.

Over the years he'd done his share of complaining about how raising his siblings had cut into his social life. He suddenly realized those fishing trips, school sporting events and even dance recitals had been the best years of his life. Until Mary Karen.

Being with her and the kids had made his life

complete. David was wrong. Travis wasn't *any-thing* like Steven.

As they headed back to Jackson in safe, dependable Ethel, a germ of an idea began to form. By the time he drove past the city limit sign, Travis knew what he was going to get M.K. for Christmas.

Something beautiful she would be proud to show off. Something practical that would make life easier. Something that would show her once and for all, that unlike her ex, being with her and the boys was the only place Travis wanted to be.

Chapter Eighteen

When Travis first mentioned celebrating Christmas in September, Mary Karen envisioned a quiet affair. They'd have takeout, the boys would open their gifts and that would be it.

Now she stood in the doorway waving goodbye to the last of family and friends who'd stop by with platters of food, bottles of wine and gifts for the boys.

Travis's hand rested lightly on her shoulder. Before the evening had begun she'd agreed to set aside her concerns for one night and enjoy the evening. And she *had* enjoyed it. He'd been by her side most of the night, greeting their guests and whispering how beautiful she looked.

Surprisingly, despite her increasing bulk, Mary Karen felt beautiful tonight. She'd twisted her hair into a stylish knot. Her new red cascade cardigan with silver threads running through it made her feel festive and fashionable. It seemed only fitting she'd have a handsome man at her side. In his chinos and brown-striped shirt, Travis made her heart go pitter-pat. Just seeing him brought a surge of possessive pride.

A possessive pride she had no right to feel.

"You were right." Mary Karen turned and pushed the door closed.

"I usually am," Travis quipped. "What was I right about this time?"

"The fishing poles. The boys loved them." She smiled, remembering their exclamations of delight. "Of course, I shouldn't have been surprised. They're still talking about last weekend's trip to the park."

"Next time, you'll have to come with us." Travis followed her to the kitchen.

Mary Karen thought about telling him there might not be a next time but instead she commandeered a half-empty bottle of sparkling grape juice from the counter and held it up. "Care to help me finish this off?"

"Absolutely." Travis grinned. "I'm into living dangerously."

Mary Karen laughed softly and emptied the bottle in the last of the clean wineglasses. "I never thought when we told people about our early Christmas that they would stop by and help us celebrate."

"I'm glad they did." Travis couldn't remember a better party. "It felt like a real holiday, having our friends and family around."

"By the end of the night, the boys were bouncing off the walls." Mary Karen placed her glass on the counter. "I'm surprised they went to bed so easily."

"I bribed them," Travis said without apology. "I told them if they went to bed without complaining, we'd go out for chocolate chip pancakes in the morning. Afterward, we'd come home and they could play with their toys."

"Sneaky." Mary Karen winked. "I like your style."

"Good." He put his glass next to hers then pulled her close. "Because I like everything about you."

"You're such a flatterer."

"Keeping it honest, babe." His arms tightened around her. "You know what it's time for?"

"More sparkling grape juice?"

Travis laughed. "Opening our gifts."

"Okay." She exhaled a breath. "Let's do it."

"Don't sound so excited," he teased, lacing his fingers through hers.

Mary Karen knew she should pull away, but

she told herself it was okay, *just for tonight.* They walked to the living room hand in hand.

The lights from the tree twinkled brightly and the delicious aroma of roasted chestnuts still lingered in the air.

"I want to open mine first," Travis said, sitting next to her on the sofa.

Despite her nervousness, Mary Karen managed to keep a smile on her face. She pointed to the gift wrapped in shiny silver paper and topped with a big red bow. "It's that one."

Travis leaned over and tugged the package out from under the tree. "This is heavy. I wonder what it is?"

He settled the gift on the coffee table in front of them. Before he could tear the package open, Mary Karen closed her hand over his arm. "I chose this gift so you'd know marriage isn't always about giving up things we love."

"Now you've piqued my curiosity." He ripped

off the paper and for a long moment simply stared.

"They're specially made for the Z4. When it's wet and sloppy outside, they'll keep your carpets dry." Mary Karen flushed, realizing Travis still hadn't said anything. Maybe he didn't like them. Maybe he didn't want ugly rubber floor mats in his expensive sports car. "I'm sorry. It was a bad idea."

"It was a very sweet thought," he said with a reassuring smile. "Thank you."

She noticed he hadn't said he liked them.

"I have the receipt in my purse," she offered, hoping he wouldn't accept. "If you want to take them back."

He just smiled and reached beneath the sofa, pulling out a box. "I have something for you."

It was smaller than the box a necklace would come in, but not as thick as ones used for rings. The paper was red-and-white stripes with a white bow, tilting slightly off center. It looked as if he'd wrapped the gift himself.

When she reached for it, he pulled the package to his chest. "Let's go outside. You can open it there."

She must have looked as confused as she felt because he smiled. "Under the moonlight will be more romantic."

Without saying another word, Travis grabbed his jacket then helped her with her coat. Taking her arm, they stepped outside and moved to the porch rail. The air was crisp but not cold. Thousands of stars filled the dark night sky. Overhead the moon cast its golden glow.

"You're right." Mary Karen put her hand on the railing and breathed in the sweet mountain air. "It's lovely out here."

"Told you so," he teased.

"Can I have my gift back now?"

He handed the package to her, his gaze as watchful as hers had been only moments before.

With trembling fingers, Mary Karen removed the wrapping and opened the box, expecting a necklace or a bracelet. Instead a fancy laser-cut key lay nestled inside.

When she made no move to take it, Travis picked it up pressed it into her palm. "With all my love."

Mary Karen cast him a curious glance. "What does it open?"

Travis gestured to a beautiful vehicle sitting in the next-door neighbor's driveway.

"Mr. and Mrs. Pettigrew's new van?"

"That's not their new van," Travis explained. "They simply let me borrow their driveway. It's *our,* or rather your, new van."

There were very few times in Mary Karen's life that she'd found herself struck dumb. This was one of them.

"I drove down to Afton to pick it up today. I thought you'd like the dark-cherry pearl color best but they said we could exchange it for another if you didn't like it." He spoke quickly, one word tumbling out after the other. "It seats eight so if we end up having another baby down the road, we'll still have room."

"You'd want another baby?"

He smiled. "I'd like to keep our options open."

She didn't know what surprised her more, that Travis had bought a minivan or that the once confirmed bachelor might want another child. She raised a hand to her head, hoping to stop the spinning. "Let me get this straight. You traded in Ethel for a new minivan?"

"Ethel isn't going anywhere." He smiled. "We need two vans, not one. I sold the Z4. You get the new van. I get Ethel. It'll take her a while to adjust, but in the end I'll win her over."

Mary Karen pulled her brows together. "But why would you get rid of your sports car?"

"You don't like the van?" Was that hurt she heard in his voice?

"Like it? I love it. Ohmigod, it's gorgeous."

Mary Karen let her gaze linger on the vehicle's sleek, modern lines. "But you've wanted that sports car for as long as I can remember. Now that you have it, why would you give it up?"

"Because I realized it's just a car." His eyes never left hers. "Having two vans will mean I can take the twins to school and pick them up. When the weather is bad you won't have to take the babies out at all."

"But taking care of the children is my job."

"It's *our* job." With gentle fingers he tucked a stray strand of hair behind her ear. "You're not alone anymore, sweetheart. You'll never be alone again. I'm not going anywhere. I'm right where I want to be, a proud member of this family."

Tears slipped down Mary Karen's cheeks. "Oh, Travis."

"I love you, M.K. The best thing I ever did was marry you in Vegas. If I had the chance, I'd do it again. I thought I had my life just the way I liked it. Until I became your husband I didn't know all that I was missing. I didn't realize that this—a home, a family and most importantly—you, my sweet wife, was exactly what I needed."

"Just having you as my husband is the only gift I need."

He lifted a brow. "Are you saying I should send the van back?"

"Not if you value your life," she warned. "Now kiss me, and then I can check out my new van."

"That's my M.K." Travis chuckled and pulled her into his arms, knowing he wouldn't want her any other way.

Epilogue

Three months later

"Sofie has my mother's red hair and fair complexion." Travis's eyes softened as he studied his newborn daughter, seemingly not bothered by her piercing cries.

"Benjamin looks a lot like your baby pictures." Mary Karen gazed at the contented baby wrapped in blue in her arms. "Speaking of pictures, take a look at the ones July dropped off. They're from Thanksgiving."

With his free hand, Travis picked up the photos lying at the end of the bed and flipped through them. A smile lifted his lips. "I like these. They're really good."

"My favorite is the one of all of us together." Mary Karen's voice grew thick with emotion. If she hadn't already known Travis loved her, the picture would have convinced her. The boys were draped all over Travis. His adoring gaze was fixed on her, his arm around her waist. Connor was making devil horns behind Travis's head. Logan had stuck his tongue out at Caleb. They were a family. A happy family.

"That picture is destined for the mantel. Until we get one that includes Ben and Sofie, that is."

"You realize Connor and Cal were counting on boys." Travis gently rocked the crying baby in his arms and raised his voice to be heard over the din.

"They'll adjust." Mary Karen knew it wouldn't

be long before the little girl had the boys eating out of her hand.

"What about her? Can you imagine what it's going to be like for her? Growing up with four older brothers?"

"Benjamin is only older by two minutes," Mary Karen pointed out.

"He's still older. Isn't he, baby girl?" Travis cooed to the red-faced infant who'd finally stopped crying to stare up at him.

"Something tells me Sofie will hold her own." Mary Karen's eyes met his. "And one day, when she's all grown up, if she's really lucky one of her brothers will have a friend. He'll be handsome and funny and smart—"

"Wait, I think I know this story," Travis interrupted, moving to his wife's side to sit beside her on the bed, his gaze never leaving hers. "They'll be best friends and then lovers. In the end they'll get married in Vegas on a wild whim and live happily ever after."

Mary Karen sighed, a wave of utter contentment washing over her. "Just like you and me."

"He'll be the luckiest guy in the world." It was all there in his eyes.

"And she'll be the luckiest woman."

Her gaze settled on Travis.

Friend. Lover. Husband. Family Man.

Who said a woman couldn't have it all?

* * * * *